DUTY

AND HONOR

DUTY
AND HONOR

A World War II Novel

Daniel Reed

iUniverse, Inc.
New York Lincoln Shanghai

DUTY AND HONOR
A World War II Novel

iUniverse, Inc.

iUniverse books may be ordered through booksellers or by contacting:

iUniverse
2021 Pine Lake Road, Suite 100
Lincoln, NE 68512
www.iuniverse.com
1-800-Authors (1-800-288-4677)

This is a work of fiction. All of the characters, names, incidents, organizations and dialogue in this novel are either the products of the author's imagination or are used fictitiously.

ISBN-13: 978-0-595-39683-2 (pbk)
ISBN-13: 978-0-595-84089-2 (ebk)
ISBN-10: 0-595-39683-6 (pbk)
ISBN-10: 0-595-84089-2 (ebk)

Printed in the United States of America

CHAPTER ONE

August 1944: A narrow sector of the imposing Eastern Front, southwestern Ukraine

Corporal Kurt Muller of the Eighty-eighth Division lay hunkered down in his trench, his thoughts drawn unavoidably to the bleakness of his situation. The German army had long since worn out its welcome, and the Great White Russian Bear was poised to deliver his final eviction notice—written in blood. As was the norm, Kurt and his comrades were up against an overwhelming Russian force.

Shells burst among the German lines, and the customary outcry of man and horse shattered the morning calm. Initially, Kurt could distinguish individual cannon fire, but soon the entire sky was ablaze with the sinister symphony of the damnable enemy artillery—jagged, knifelike shrapnel killing and maiming at will. Deafening explosions forged moonlike craters, instantly entombing comrades up and down the line.

As the guns fell silent, Russian infantry sprang from their entrenchments, spearheaded by penal battalions employed as minesweepers to preserve the invaluable tanks. It was first light and time God Almighty turned his attention elsewhere while his most cherished creations treated one another in a way he never planned.

Kurt's mind drifted to the summer of '41, when he and the Nazi legions had advanced without respite through these same fields. He never imagined that one day he'd be on his heels, dragging his wounded comrades and shattered pride toward the very extremities of the Fatherland. A sense of impending ruin had long since supplanted the rush of their awe-inspiring *blitzkrieg*. The German invaders awaited the retribution to come in the slaughterhouse known as the Russian Front.

Kurt wondered how he would survive the day's bloodletting. Becoming a prisoner of war simply wasn't an option. Better a Russian bullet or bayonet to cut short this nightmare. Better even to take his own life, as so many comrades had.

Mere words could never do justice to such widespread despair and all-consuming fatalism. Unbridled fear governed the thought process, though Kurt found it most difficult to conceive his own demise. A minor abrasion—even a serious one—was thinkable, but he simply could not imagine the cold lumps of dirt dropping on his lifeless form.

The steady rumble of onrushing Soviet T-34s combined with the incessant shelling to reduce the earth to a shuddering mass of uncertainty. As the howl of enemy infantry drew near, Kurt yearned with an unearthly passion to run from the unceasing affliction. But he'd not shirk his duty. He'd make his stand there in that dark and dismal ditch, for that was his destiny, his calling, his obligation to his country.

Never before that mournful day had he felt so hopeless. What if he did not survive the day? His remains would be left to rot and decay with no thought of burial.

Kurt's thoughts shifted to his best friend, Arie Schonert, with whom he had served shoulder to shoulder from the onset of his enlistment. He was in the next trench over, assigned to watch over a raw recruit. As was the custom prior to a major engagement, Kurt had exchanged a letter home with Arie, should one outlast the other.

Thoughts of his cherished family prompted him to reach with trembling fingers for the precious letter. Lovingly unfolding and resting it upon unsteady knees, he read again his parents' love and concern. His mother wrote, "We are praying every day for your safe return. We miss you and long to see you again. Are you eating well?"

Kurt realized how badly he wanted to survive—needed to survive—no matter how decidedly dismal his existence might be. If but for the sake of his precious family he had to outlast this madness and go home to them. He longed to know the joys of falling in love, of becoming a loving and caring father like his own, of reuniting with his parents in their beloved land. The ongoing death and misery in Russia had taught him that life is precious and must go on, in spite of his present circumstances.

A shell from a T-34 sprayed great clumps of earth and rock upon him, wresting the treasured correspondence from his lap. He retrieved it but dared not read on, and he struggled to prevent tears of self-pity from spilling down his cheeks. In his return letter he had, once again, judiciously camouflaged the ghastly reality of his unbearable conditions and the unending peril.

Kurt returned the letter to his shirt pocket as another shell burst nearby, shaking the ground beneath him and adding to the terror that was steadily overtaking and eroding what was left of his sanity. The enemy's Katyusha rockets, "Stalin's Organs," propagated unbridled fear in the ranks even before the actual impact. No matter how many of these tragic life-and-death confrontations he had survived—and there were many—he suffered the same gut-wrenching unrest that had characterized his initial engagement three summers past.

As Kurt thrust his forefingers deep into his aching ears and awaited the next round of nerve-shattering horror in the form of the stampeding Soviets, he reflected on his most enjoyable childhood pastime—play-fighting with neighborhood chums, wielding sculpted sticks for rifles and potatoes for grenades. He recalled his incessant reading of the accounts of awe-inspiring conflicts from the past—the famous and heroic campaigns of Alexander, Napoleon, and Frederick the Great. He had even managed to concoct a few of his own along the way. Dashing home from school to sit at the kitchen table with pen and paper, he had conjured up battles with heroes strong and brave, never imagining the incalculable agony that goes hand in glove with such magnificent exploits. Fantasies that as a child had been so innocent and so much fun now appalled him.

He thought of the childhood ambitions that had occupied his imaginative mind in those carefree days: doctor, fireman, minister, architect, pilot, scientist, policeman—back when he dared to dream beyond surviving the day. Such optimism was gone for good by 1944. His singular fantasy now lay in outlasting the absurdity and returning home to an honest job, any job, no matter how menial or mundane.

With the unholy shrillness of the onrushing Soviets pounding in his ears, Kurt bowed his head one last time to plead for deliverance. "Father, into your hands I commit my spirit."

A comrade wailed for a medic above the inexorable din of battle, bringing Kurt's invocation to a fitting conclusion. Gathering the courage to emerge from his trench, he beheld the carcasses of numerous T-34s smoldering in the distance. He noted with admiration the effectiveness of the land mines and 88 mm anti-tank guns, which had somehow survived the thunderous artillery barrage. Next the German howitzers and *Nebelwerfer* rockets began exacting a demanding toll on the unsheltered brown wave of infantry gallantly pressing toward them. To his right, Kurt distinguished several of their own Panther and Tiger tanks entering the fray, combining with small-arms fire and heavy machine guns to spew out wholesale death and dismemberment to the hated Reds.

A seedling of hope grew in Kurt's heart as hundreds of the shadowy figures converging upon them fell to the shattered earth, the sharp screams of the dying nearly drowning out the noise of the weaponry. The forepart of a Soviet tank blew skyward when its treads hit a mine; munitions and petrol ignited, unleashing a sensational sheet of flame. Through the amassing smoke and dust, hand-to-hand skirmishes broke out as the Communists reached the forward trenches. Kurt recoiled to see a comrade ingested by the treads of a T-34.

"Muller," came a scratchy utterance to his left, the man inching his way toward him, his eyes wide as saucers, terror oozing from every pore. "My name is Wild…Gunter Wild, from Rohrbach's squad. I'm told you're a deeply religious man, Muller. You must promise to pray for me; I've got such a bad feeling for this one…. I'm not much on speaking terms with him," he explained, his blood-shot eyes lifting toward heaven, "or I'd do it myself. All right?"

"All right," Kurt answered, grasping his arm. "I'd be glad to represent you, Gunter Wold, but I'm sure he'd love to hear from you, too."

"Wild. Wild with an *i*!" he exclaimed, nose and eyes flaring. "Gunter Wild!"

"OK, Wild, consider it done," Kurt assured him, closing his eyes and mumbling a prayer as the man slithered back to his post.

A second later Kurt was on his feet, his 8 mm taking on a life of its own. He became a man possessed in his white-knuckled battle for survival. Love of the glorious Fatherland and the once-blessed *Führer*, near the forefront of his motivation short years before, meant little now. What pugnacity he had left was strictly personal.

The Russians' forward lines were all but decimated—swept away like dust. As sporadic survivors came into range, both sides unleashed grenades. The Russkies took to the air like gymnasts, wrenching and writhing in agony. An explosion to Kurt's left dispatched him to his knees beneath a deluge of convulsed earth. He beheld Gunter Wild wild-eyed and pulsating in unimaginable agony against the back wall of the trench, gaping incredulously at the stub that seconds ago was his left arm. A medic was on the scene at once, dressing the hideous wound and attempting to restore a semblance of calm to the poor fellow, who was enveloped in the clenches of potentially fatal shock.

Kurt found his feet in time to encounter a shabby and unshaven enemy soldier, dreadfully bloodied but very much alive, lunging at him with a fixed bayonet and a half-crazed shriek terrifying enough to wake the dead. The whites of his bullish eyes were streaked with a mix of hate and horror. Kurt lurched to the right, then reached instinctively for the trenching tool about his waist. In an instant, his assailant lay dead, his blood showering Kurt's face.

Kurt gawked savage-eyed into the gathering furor. Whether it had been chance or divine providence that had thus far seen him through, he could not say, but he was most grateful.

Sweat dripped freely from Kurt's chin. It seemed the very air about him was ablaze as the fighting reached its climax. He observed the wounded foes squirming and groaning in their acute misery, a bona fide banquet of misfortune. One man extended his arm, begging for a bullet, but Kurt was altogether too preoccupied with his own private hell to sympathize with these miserable wretches.

Then, profusely accented with profanity, came the dreaded signal from the company commander: the beckoning for a counterattack.

Kurt reluctantly fixed his bayonet to his rifle with unsteady hands. He dragged himself from the comparative sanctuary of his entrenchment and set out to direct his squad ahead. He attempted to rouse his courage with a death-defying war cry, but no sound came from his fright-filled lungs. He felt like a child.

Kurt recognized a young man from his squad, Karl Eckhart, cowering in his dugout, whimpering uncontrollably, his pants soaked with piss. As his squad leader, it was Kurt's responsibility to get him up and moving to avoid a firing squad.

"Get up, Karl. We're going forward," he screamed.

"I can't. I just can't!" Eckhart wailed.

Two violent smashes from Kurt's open hand brought him to his senses, and Kurt callously ordered him to his feet while gripping the back of his tunic. Forcing the young man's rifle into his quaking hands and goading him along, Kurt raced forward, inserting a fresh clip into his weary weapon.

Kurt fully understood Eckhart's fear, and it brought to mind his favorite Psalm: "Yea, though I walk through the valley of the shadow of death, I will fear no evil; for thou art with me; thy rod and thy staff they comfort me." Yet the fear was there—a shuddering, all-pervading fear.

Kurt passed a multitude of mangled bodies—dead and otherwise—strewn along the smoke-filled, stricken battlefield; their blood and innards littering the landscape. The roar of battle was altogether deafening. Bullets bit into the earth, and men struck by enemy fire fell with a shriek or dull groan. Yet he pressed on into the thick of the fighting where the cratered battlefield was even more congested with the dead and dying and the wailing wounded. When bullets ran out, men resorted to bayonets and bare hands. A comrade roared past at a gallop, ranting and raving with arms flailing, clearly gone mad from the unmerciful bombing and bloodshed. The fearsome clamor and chaos of battle, together with the repugnant spectacle, heightened Kurt's anxiety. He peered frantically through the smoke, fully expecting at any moment to be blown to bits or shot clean through the heart. He prayed, "God, end it mercifully, if this is my time!"

Thankfully, the Soviets were attempting to retire en masse, leaving behind sporadic, scattered pockets of suicidal resistance. Kurt's gaze fell upon a dismembered enemy soldier exhibiting the death-like stupor he had grown so used to seeing. Kurt pondered that this young man, too, had a mother and father at home praying for his safe return.

Suddenly, a pistol shot rang out—thankfully errant—from a fallen Soviet not ten paces to Kurt's left. A heavy-bearded officer with much of his upper torso drenched in blood had fired on him. Kurt aimed his 8 mm and let fly; the poor devil's head snapped backward, quickly ending his ill-fated journey.

Ahead to the right, Kurt spied a machine gun and mortar position, a rear guard to shield the Russian withdrawal. Favorably sheltered, it was dealing out death and mutilation with nearly every burst. Kurt and his men were in position to deliver enfilade fire but, by closing the distance, they could be more effective. Keeping a wary eye out for further enemy threats, Kurt advanced, flanked by Eckhart and Arie. It was not until they were within a stone's throw that they were spotted, and the Russians frantically pivoted to allot them their undivided attention. As if synchronized, Kurt and the others unleashed three grenades, blasting the enemies out of their boots and putting an immediate end to the Soviet opposition.

Kurt and his compatriots lay motionless, cautiously surveying the area for additional pockets of unrest. Hosts of men from both sides lay inanimate, while others thrashed about in their grief.

German troops were up and in full stride, mopping up the last of the Russians and gathering a few prisoners along the way. Shots rang out when the enemy's seriously wounded were eliminated—seemingly a harsh measure, but in fact decidedly humane.

The commander employed his whistle. "Regroup. Fall back," he shouted.

Some of the men paused to assist the grievously overburdened medical orderlies with the myriad of wounded, many of whom slithered about, suffused with pain, as they dragged themselves to the safety of their lines. Among the casualties was Kurt's own Dieter Braun, a seasoned soldier of middle age who had been called up to fill the conspicuous void left by the costly loss of so many of the nation's young men. Braun was being hoisted onto a worn-out stretcher, and he audibly suffered from a grotesque wound to his left hip.

Kurt sought attention for a minor abrasion above the left ear, likely a shrapnel wound.

Arie cleaned the wound and wrapped a dressing about his friend's head.

Kurt could account for all but one of his men, prompting him to search the slain. He discovered the hollow-eyed Willi Zillstra, a fresh recruit of seventeen with scarcely a week in the field. His mouth, cavernous as though awestruck, gaped to reveal the violence of his passing. He was entangled with a lifeless Russian in the posture of lovers, each having mortally bludgeoned the other. Like so many of the youngsters before him who were snatched from their mothers and fitted for the uniform, Zillstra had been deemed expendable by a heartless regime. Cheated of his precious youth, he'd been flung heedlessly into the blasting furnace that consumed mere boys before they had even begun to experience all that this life has to offer.

CHAPTER TWO

Still reeling from the barbaric butchery, Kurt realized he needed to relax and collect what was left of his waning sanity. He contemplated the letter he would dispatch to Willi's parents. Though it was officially the responsibility of the unit commander to notify them of his loss, Kurt felt compelled to add his sincere condolences. As he scanned the pathetic battleground, its tanks aflame amid corpses lying thick as grass, he imagined he could use the bodies as stepping stones and march clear to the Russian lines, never bringing his foot down on Mother Earth. What carnage! The keepers of heaven and hell would be well-occupied this day.

As an ugly curtain of smoke and dust settled over the tortured battlescape, Kurt dug into his rucksack to look at priceless photos of family and friends and to make note of the battle in his diary. He had outlived yet another brush with death. Thank God! He speculated that the Almighty must have some special purpose for his life, and he bowed in thanksgiving.

It was time to painstakingly record details of this latest installment in his continuing misadventure. He noted that creatures of the so-called lower order, the animals and birds, had had the common sense to flee this disturbing insanity, while man seemed everlastingly beguiled and drawn to it like flies to dung. He looked out as a living witness to the futility of war. Where was the glory here? As the horrifying outcry of the wounded lying unattended between the battle lines stabbed at his crippled senses, Kurt pondered that the only creatures to profit from this day were the maggots and flies and assorted scavengers. Reflecting on the torn landscape before him, he perceived that the once-enchanting panorama of days gone by was now but an eerie testament to what the Good Book refers to as the innate depravity of man. He sat amidst a picture postcard of the abyss itself, surrounded by severed tree trunks that rose from a cursed, cancerous soil.

Kurt thumbed through the tattered pages of his diary, recalling the Old Testament passage which so aptly depicted his ordeal: "There is a right time for everything: a time to be born and a time to die; a time to plant and a time to harvest; a time to kill and a time to heal; a time to destroy and a time to rebuild; a time to cry and a time to laugh; a time to grieve and a time to dance; a time for scattering stones and a time for gathering stones; a time to embrace and a time not to embrace; a time to find and a time to lose; a time for keeping and a time for throwing away; a time to tear and a time to repair; a time to be quiet and a time to speak up; a time for loving and a time for hating; a time for war and a time for peace."

As Kurt deliberated upon these timeless words of wisdom, he thought how they provided a fitting summary to his difficult life as a young man searching for meaning and order in a world largely void of it. He was a soldier, now a veteran, of the German army. Like so many young men of his time, he'd been swept up in the horrific and senseless fighting tearing apart whole nations and killing millions of human beings during its inglorious run.

Not surprisingly, the diary contained vivid accounts of the victorious months early in the conflict and tapered off afterward. Drunk with irrepressible power and driven by stunning success, the German army literally swaggered through the opening months of the Russian campaign with never a thought of defeat. Indestructible, it had the entire world at its feet.

As he continued paging through the diary, he read the entries from Kiev in early September of that victorious season. There he had witnessed a sight so spectacular it defied adequate description: a deluge of incinerated and disemboweled Soviet trucks and tanks scattered across acres of burnt, once-lush cropland. Clusters of field guns and gigantic heaps of rifles lay abandoned, along with the mangled and mutilated carcasses of the hapless Soviet soldiers. Most magnificent of all was the spectacle of an endless column of distraught enemy prisoners—some three-quarters of a million men—winding their way with the compliance of a primary school fire drill toward a most uncertain future. The irony of it all was that, though he failed to comprehend it at the time, Kurt was every bit as much a captive as they, having been called to surrender his very life and its attending liberties to a cause he couldn't even understand, let alone consent to.

For the ensuing three years, he had been caught up in the most unimaginable horror that could befall a man. Mental anguish, physical discomfort, and unbri-

dled fear and loathing had been his constant companions as his two-year obligation to the military extended nearly beyond his endurance.

He and his comrades had marched and fought week after week and month
after month, slaying and taking captive vast numbers of Russian soldiers—only to
discover there were always more to take their place. The Soviets gamely absorbed
the invading troops into their expansive domain like a sponge, willing to concede
men and precious land for still more precious time—time to strengthen and prepare for the coming counterstrike.

Perpetually disheartened and worn to a frazzle, the German fighting men
turned to vodka and cognac to combat their pathetic reality. They were forever
dirty, reeking, and unshaven, lacking the basic rudiments of medical care. Often
sick in body and spirit, and badly in need of rest and even hospitalization, they
were instead called upon to advance or retreat, fight, and subsist on bad food and
meager shelter.

Kurt had attended to the misfortune of more than one man who had been left
lying by the roadside or in a trench during one of their many withdrawals; these
men had pleaded for a merciful end to their pitiful lives, preferring death to Russian captivity. He had observed the treatment of human beings, both civilian and
military, not at all unlike that meted out to unsavory creatures such as rats. He
understood now that there could be no full recovery from the emotional and
mental torments he had been subjected to for so long on the stony Eastern Front.
Oh, that he could be stricken with amnesia!

During his enlistment he had witnessed, time and again, the stark contrasts
between feats of remarkable courage and willful cowardice, noble comradeship
and disturbing self-centeredness, heartfelt sensitivity and ruthless savagery, and
striking beauty and scenes so repulsive as to compel the devil himself to turn his
head. He had come to learn that warfare, much like his childhood soccer
matches, was not nearly so agreeable when one was on the losing side.

Kurt was well aware of the mournful wartime plight of defenseless women and
children; he knew these innocents had been mistreated too. But the incalculable
woe of the enlisted man was not exactly an enviable one. He was every bit as
much a victim of the tragic inhumanity brought on by these violent confrontations between embattled nations and their unfit warlords. More often than not, it
was the enlisted man who was called upon to pay the ultimate sacrifice.

How many women and children, no matter how unpleasant their circumstances, were obliged to undergo the day-to-day hardships common to the fighting man, such as sleeping and eating in the mud and filth of crude shelters? How
many of them were driven relentlessly—like beasts of burden—through the para-

lyzing severity of the savage Russian winter, with its near-total incapacitation of men and machines? Temperatures of thirty degrees below zero, common in the dead of a Russian winter, chill clean through to the soul and often result in excruciating frostbite and amputation.

Have the noncombatants known the arduous demands of forced marches? Have they engaged the enemy while disregarding the tormenting thorn of near-starvation, when a head of cabbage or a slab of aged horse flesh would be received with all the enthusiasm of a four-course gourmet meal? And what of the afflictions of rampant disease and the scourge of lice and vermin which are the soldier's common portion?

Governed by such dog-eat-dog conditions, it was practically impossible for a man to extend his concerns to those around him; he became a veritable monument to self-centeredness and self-indulgence, quite able to dispassionately observe and walk past settings of immeasurable misery.

As for their adversary, Ivan was a total mystery. On the one hand, he could cravenly unite with a half million of his comrades in utter capitulation to trod off into a hopeless captivity; on the other, he could resist with unmatched gallantry to the bitter end.

Like Napoleon's presumptuous legions before them, the German army pranced dutifully into the vastness of Russia, only to be brutally stymied by its pitiless winter and unyielding populace. There seemed to be absolutely no end to this unbearable country. The farther they advanced, the more precarious their condition, and they existed in perpetual dread of a Russian rebound.

More as a result of Kurt's lengthy service than of any innate or acquired leadership qualities, he had been promoted to corporal in December 1942. His predecessor, a rather foul-mannered and universally disdained character, had been found lifeless in his trench, a casualty of what seemed their number one nemesis, the relentlessly inhumane winter weather. They had no sooner entombed him in his trench than his lieutenant had informed Kurt of the promotion.

Kurt's eyes tightened in painful recollection upon perusing the pages that recounted the dreadful midsummer of 1943, when his division had been cast into the apocalyptic cauldron known as the Battle of Kursk. Tanks and human beings had been willfully sacrificed as never before in a bid to turn back the overwhelming tide of Russian resurgence. The German million-man offensive failed to faze the ever-improving Soviets. Taken together with the staggering expenditure of one-quarter of a million comrades at Stalingrad the previous winter, the losses at Kursk meant that the forlorn fate of the German army was thus sealed, marking the complete end of its Eastern aspirations.

Most depressing of all was Kurt's entry about his division being all but deci-mated in early February of 1944, when a massive Soviet offensive had encircled them outside the Ukrainian town of Cherkassy. Only a daring and costly break-out under cover of darkness had saved them from the much-dreaded horrors of Soviet capture, a fate feared worse than death. Their flight from this calamity had included a headlong dash with Soviet tanks nipping at their heels. The weak and wounded had been left to the mercy—or rather the malignity—of their pursuers, and Kurt remembered fleeing as if among a frenzied herd of African wildebeest. Hurling themselves without hesitation into a river covered with a thin sheet of ice, they had reckoned that to drown or die of hypothermia would be the least of many evils. Hundreds succumbed to the icy waters and many more to the aveng-ing Soviets, who made sport of their dire predicament.

Morale was a distant memory in those days of defeat and retreat, though the German army maintained its discipline and a remnant of its courage. Nerves were frazzled, and hope for a bright future was long gone. Nevertheless, like the hand-carved toy soldiers who had died a thousand gruesome deaths in Kurt's backyard sandbox, they kept coming back for more. And there was always more.

Kurt ran a hand through the thick brown hair atop his handsome, weathered face before returning the diary to his sack. His appearance suggested innocence and tenderness, qualities at total odds with the brutal warrior he'd been forced to become to survive the Eastern Front. He'd never been a brawny sort, but three years on a survival diet had left him strong and wiry with not a pound of excess weight.

His squad gathered in dusty, ragged attire, their visages displaying an unattrac-tive mix of blood, sweat, and dust. He was reminded again of their warm bond and single-minded loyalty. They were younger than he, and most of them were considerably less experienced. He had become more than their superior in the field of battle by demonstrating a genuine concern for them as individuals and teaching them vital rules of survival. Their undeniable respect for him as their corporal and squad leader was appreciated, but he prized their daily camaraderie most. As he looked out over the unburied glut of decaying and bloating remains, he was thankful his squad's losses were comparatively light.

They had been spared Russian air strikes, but the day was young. The glorious *blitzkrieg* of yesteryear now long gone, the German air force was routinely out-numbered five to one.

The ration kits were soon exhausted as the men sought to replenish the con-siderable energy spent in the early morning struggle. They shared accounts of the bloody battle with an energized dignity bordering on conceit. Drawing heavily on cigarettes, each one strove to outdo the others.

With an empty plate at his feet and a cigarette in the corner of his mouth, Arie proudly displayed a bullet hole through the armpit of his shirt. "Hey, look here, boys. Am I living a charmed life or what?" At twenty-two, a year older than Kurt, Arie had lost the tip of his left ear to frostbite during the first winter. A hero sort who had distinguished himself time and again, he had been awarded the coveted Iron Cross one winter's day for his daring elimination of two onrushing T-34s. Square-jawed, blond-haired, blue-eyed, muscle-bound, and sure-fire handsome, if only ruggedly so, Arie could well have been a *Wehrmacht* poster boy. Less than average in height but pugnacious to the core, he'd been likened to a two-legged pit bull. Intensity and anger had brought him two promotions in his initial six months on the front; the same intensity and anger had wiped them out in a two-minute tirade. Quiet but not unsociable, Arie was at times very difficult to reach but always worth the effort.

The revelry took Kurt back to his secondary school graduation party; though not too distant in the past, it seemed a decade ago. So enraptured from having survived yet another hellish battle, the men carried on as though they'd all been granted honorable discharges.

One of the men looked over his shoulder at the smoldering carnage and asked, "Do you think they'll come back at us again today, Arie?"

"I wouldn't put it past them," he answered. "That could've been a first wave to soften us up. If nothing else, we'll get it from their artillery."

Kurt suddenly took to his feet. "Attention," he barked upon the arrival of their long-legged company commander, Captain Rademaker.

The captain was a kind and considerate officer, not of the hardened Nazi class the men had come to despise. Never far from the booze, he had confessed to having willfully crawled deep into a bottle of cognac—with but few brief and unhappy periods of sobriety—the moment he had set foot on Russian soil. He had refused to come out until this thing was over. A self-admitted coward from stem to stern, Rademaker had no delusions of grandeur, and he fully intended to share his experiences with his grandchildren. He once quipped that he was the only soldier to see the same bullet twice: once when it passed him and again when he passed the bullet. This restrained demeanor was unmistakable in his laid-back leadership, which was rarely exemplary.

"At ease, men," he offered, scratching his stubbled face. "I should think you've been uneasy enough for one day." Pausing to lift one foot up on an ammunition box, he continued, "It appears we've weathered the storm and put the royal boots to Ivan. I don't suspect the fornicators are up for another mauling anytime soon, but do be on your guard."

He addressed Kurt directly. "Your losses, Corporal."

Kurt handed him Zillstra's ID tags. "One dead, one wounded, sir."

"Not bad, Muller. Not bad at all. Not every squad in my command was that fortunate."

"No, sir. We were very lucky indeed."

"And allow me to personally commend you for your assault on that Russian machine gun position. You men saved many lives with that heroic thrust."

Kurt broke a smile. "Thank you, Captain."

"I'd like a word with you and Private Schonert," he said.

Kurt and Arie followed the captain a short distance, expecting to be enjoined to some perilous mission.

Rademaker addressed them in a serous vein. "I've just received some very important news from division. You two are being directed to march to the train station at Bessarabka and initiate a ten-day leave from active service, beginning immediately." A broad smirk traveled across his face as he reached inside his briefcase for the furlough papers. "Division is finally offering you leave, men. Well deserved and overdue."

Kurt and Arie couldn't believe their luck. They embraced Rademaker, abandoning protocol by carrying on with him as one would a school chum.

Rademaker turned to leave, raising his voice with the requisite reminders. "Wash yourselves. You smell like pigs. Shave, and draw clean uniforms from supply."

A marvelous tide of joy washed over Kurt as he contemplated his trip home. He envisioned a smothering, front yard reception followed by hour after hour of blissful fellowship, untroubled serenity, and blessed rest and relaxation far from this insufferable place.

Kurt said, "I must check on Braun before we go, Arie. You get cleaned up, and we'll meet back here within the hour. OK?"

"You got it," Arie answered. "And don't be gone long, or I swear I'll leave without you."

CHAPTER THREE

Kurt hastily gathered his gear and headed to the rear, where he would effect a quick—and yet comforting—visit to a fallen compatriot likely facing a leg amputation. The lone ray of light in Braun's cheerless state was the contemplation of a one-way ticket home to sit out the balance of this heinous conflict. On the surface, Kurt wondered whether to extend pity or to envy the man, but deep down he knew Braun was much worse off than himself.

Fritz Becker, the squad radio operator and close friend of Dieter Braun's, called out, "Kurt, I'd like to tag along to the infirmary."

"I welcome your company," Kurt answered, "but no more than five minutes and then we're out of there."

Downright skinny and built short to the ground, the straitlaced, bookish Becker was a devout Lutheran boy from a dumpy little Prussian town. As such, he made for a comforting soul mate.

They presently happened upon some hapless prisoners from the German counterattack who were awaiting transport to the prison camps. Kurt drew his companion's attention to a dark and mustached man looking like a dead man walking. The Russian's right cheek was shaped like a grapefruit by an outrageous wad of snuff, and he was in noticeable distress. He apparently was hiding a serious wound to avoid being shot. "Look at that poor devil," Kurt said. "His right arm is a bloody pulp."

"Yes," answered Becker, "and like so many of his unfortunate countrymen before him, he can expect absolutely no medical services from his captors. Man's will to survive is truly remarkable."

Kurt nodded. "Particularly in this hellhole."

The men detected in the captives a blend of dishonor, hate, anxiety, and gloom.

Kurt was deeply sorry for what his people had brought upon the Russians and their beautiful land. In the trenches, the only emotions he seemed capable of were wholesale fear and malice, but in scenes like this he saw the enemy as hopeless, helpless victims of a fraudulent and shamefully unjust system. Not unlike those of German soldiers, Russian lives were thoughtlessly forfeited—and always for, at best, an exceptionally perplexing and dubious rationale. A soldier no more willingly forfeits his life for his country than a deer lays down its life to feed the hunter's family.

Coming upon the grief-stricken infirmary, Kurt steeled himself against what he knew would be utterly repugnant to each and every one of his senses. The gruesome sights and putrid smells were barely tolerable, but it was the insufferable sounds of men writhing in such profound agony that distressed him more each time he made a joyless visit to these miserable quarters. Several covered corpses offered a pathetic glimpse of what lay ahead. As he gazed at the inanimate shapes that just awhile ago were walking, talking, and breathing human beings with hopes and dreams like his own, he reflected on his miserable vulnerability.

The infirmary was, of course, a veritable beehive, the blood-blanketed medical personnel perspiring profusely beneath an unbearable workload. Usually, Kurt would have waited a few hours for the turmoil ensuing a major battle to subside, but with him leaving within the hour, it was then or never.

He turned to Becker. "Remember, we mustn't be long here."

The men recoiled from the unsettling murmur of flies as they advanced through rows of suffering soldiers. They cringed at the sharp, shrill cries of pain that punctured the air. Most were mere boys in men's clothing. The desperate fighting had taken a tremendous toll on the country's menfolk, and it appeared that Hitler was now dispatching the next generation to hold the much-maligned Commies at bay. They paused to yield the right-of-way to two orderlies who were transferring an exceptionally young recruit to the surgeon's table. Blood red from chest to knees, the youngster covered a gaping abdominal wound with his quivering hands, while his face reflected extreme terror.

"Why do they bother sending us these adolescents?" Becker moaned with upturned hands. "They never last the first month, and they're no good to us at any rate."

"I hear you," Kurt answered. "Sorrowful fatality rate among these kids, but I'm afraid it'll only get worse."

They couldn't help noticing the visible agony and despair of those stretched out on rickety tables and cots and filth-ridden floors, a suffering only the horrid spectacle of death could alleviate. Men agonized over the loss of an arm or leg, and others suffered horribly crushed skulls or repulsive facial lacerations, while still more lay in hopeless misery from hideous chest and stomach wounds. Kurt considered that these shattered individuals were not the senseless, unfeeling farm beasts he'd helped butcher as a lad, but rather emotional, responsive human beings steeped in hellish torment. Their eyes betrayed their contemplation of the terrifying blackness of death, the inevitability of never again seeing cherished family and sweethearts who loved them dearly and longed desperately for their safe return.

They came upon a familiar face, and Kurt reached to grasp Braun's quivering hand.

Braun managed an anxious smile. A tear streamed down his left cheek as he struggled not to cry out against his oppressive pain and his miserable circumstance.

Subdued with sorrow and sympathy for this brave and blameless individual, Kurt asked, "Can you stand the pain, Dieter? Should I have an orderly bring some morphine?"

But Braun was largely incoherent; the inquiry fell upon deaf ears.

They visited a short while, but Braun drifted in and out of consciousness and labored so in pain that the visitors decided to make their exit; but first, Kurt gently took Braun's hand in his and pledged to keep him in his thoughts and prayers in the days ahead. Amazingly, the sum total of the incalculable death and misery this horrific hostility had heaped upon him had yet to shatter his faith in a higher power, and he resolved to plead daily for his comrade's recovery.

Braun slowly raised his head to gaze at his wound, sweat dripping from his forehead. "I'm done for, Kurt. I'd sooner be dead than a cripple the rest of my life, anyway. I'm resigned to it." He clenched Kurt's forearm. "Promise me you'll write my wife and kids." He paused. "Tell them how much I love them." Tears spilled down his cheeks. "Promise me."

Kurt's reply was warmly reassuring. "You'll be able to write them yourself, and you don't know that you'll be a cripple anyway. I recovered from a leg wound like yours. But yes, I promise to write your loved ones to let them know about your wound."

On the way out Becker spat, "I hate this stinking war and the lunatics who brought it upon us. May Hitler and his cronies be stricken with an incurable disease and rot in hell."

"You think you're unearthing some novel perspective there, Becker?" Kurt asked.

Becker grabbed Kurt's arm as they passed a medical cart laden with morphine, gauze, and disinfectants. "Kurt, the wounded Russian in the yard. What do you say?"

"Don't even think about it. I've seen men shot for less."

Becker swallowed hard, strode toward the cart like he owned it, and began packing his pockets.

Though Kurt was tempted to scold his subordinate and send him back to the cart with the medications, his heart won out over his mind. He followed Becker's lead out the door, yielding to a heaving truckload of wooden coffins.

They came upon the Russians being herded onto several badly overcrowded transports. Becker meandered into the pack, searching for the injured man. He found him slumped against a truck, shoving a revolting black blotch of snuff back into his mouth with the back of a hairy hand.

Kurt scanned the area fretfully, on the lookout for the heartless SS guards in charge of transferring the prisoners. If caught handing out precious German first aid to the enemy, Becker would find himself in a world of distress.

The prisoner hesitated at first, but ultimately he accepted the supplies with a degree of uncertainty.

Kurt was charged with joy at the spectacle of the suffering man's smile. Warmheartedly, he formed a fist and punched at Becker's shoulder as they hustled back to the squad. Suddenly the two were chilled to the very bone by a commotion at the trucks. One of the Ukrainian sentries enlisted to tend the POWs had blown the whistle on Becker for his benevolent act. The two were unceremoniously stopped in their tracks and brought to attention to confront a seriously distraught, beefy-faced SS lieutenant who wore a patch over one eye. He had recovered the first aid and, along with the maimed prisoner, strode toward them, broadcasting a withering glare. At the very least, they were in for one dickens of a tongue-lashing.

Kurt's mind retreated to a dismal setting near Kharkov prior to Christmas of '43, where two half-starved comrades had been shot—without benefit of a court-martial—for breaking into the depleted supply depot to appease their penetrating hunger. He suffered a sudden stab of anxiety; beads of perspiration formed on his forehead, his palms grew clammy, and trickles of sweat ran down his arms.

The veins in his neck bulging like a fat woman's girdle, the officer was exceedingly exasperated over Becker's philanthropic gesture. He straightaway thundered out a severe reprimand laced with a storm of expletives over the squandering of German supplies on this worthless creature.

Becker said, "It was all my doing, Herr Lieutenant. Corporal Muller did all he could to restrain me."

Kurt countered, "I am as guilty as he, sir. I must be called to account for my inaction. Please, Lieutenant, sir, I appeal for leniency. We've been under intense pressure for many weeks without adequate rest."

His face one big scowl, the SS officer stepped closer, and Kurt withered under the foul, sewer-smelling breath that reeked of garlic and hygienic neglect. "We are all under intense pressure, Corporal," he bawled in a cackling voice, "but that does not excuse such a serious breakdown in discipline! There are spectators to this treacherous act who are wondering how the German army deals with such thievery. They shall soon find out!"

Kurt appealed to the man's sense of humanity, though he sensed it was entirely futile, given the intolerant mindset of this pompous ass. "Herr Lieutenant, Private Becker was merely extending to this man the consideration I would wish upon every German soldier in the enemy's POW camps. The prisoner has a severe wound and is in considerable pain. He might have bled to death or died of infection without the supplies."

Immersed in a keep-your-mouth-shut countenance, the lieutenant thundered, "The penalty for theft of state property is death." He drew his pistol and aimed it at Kurt's forehead.

Kurt wondered if this was how he would meet his end after three hellish years on the ruthless Russian Front.

The officer lowered the firearm, directed it at the prisoner, and—without taking his eyes off Kurt—gunned the man down with no more sentiment than one would swat a fly.

Kurt stared in disbelief at the lieutenant and then at the pitiful sight staining the dirt at his feet: a creature who made one final, agonizing gasp before moving on to what was hopefully a better state. Kurt marveled at the epidemic inhumanity generated by this dreadful conflict that had transformed many into a form more animal than human.

As he holstered his pistol, the lieutenant had the look of having righted a great wrong by substituting for Kurt's death the death of this wretched Russian. Brandishing a sullied agglomeration of craggy yellow teeth, the officer snorted, "Lucky for you, I am reluctant to sacrifice men from the front line in such desperate times. I will spare your pitiful lives solely for the sake of the blessed Fatherland. You, Corporal, are dismissed. I will deal further with the thief. Notify your company commander that this man will be put to good use for the next few days on burial detail. He'll be made available should the enemy resume its offensive."

As he turned to leave, Kurt exchanged wounded glances with an expressionless Becker, wondering what could possibly account for the unbridled malignity displayed by so many officers toward the enlisted men. The belligerence of the Russian combatants and the ruthlessness of the merciless partisans concealed in the forested hill country were no puzzle, but that of their own officers was hard to fathom. The rank and file were always getting the dirty end of the stick.

CHAPTER FOUR

After a most rudimentary splashdown with cold water, Kurt and Arie drew furlough pay, new uniforms, soap, foot powder, socks, cigarettes, blanket rolls, and bread bags. The field kitchen provided many luxuries for their auspicious journey, including sardines, biscuits, chocolate, bacon, and schnapps. After all, the home front must not see its servicemen returning in faded uniforms and deficient of needed supplies.

The squad members gathered for a proper send-off, genuinely happy for their veteran comrades, who were long overdue a trip home.

The dusty road leading from the front lines to the train station was like a pathway to heaven itself. Their homes and families functioned as lighthouses from which nothing could deter them. They set off in good humor buoyed by the highest of spirits, passing a monotoned officer lecturing a company of baby-faced recruits on the need to stop the Communist aggressor from enslaving the German people.

Arie shook his head and sneered, "No one will ever know how much I hate these degenerate Nazis. Their half-baked propaganda makes me want to retch. The unsympathetic officers and bloodsucking bureaucrats are always being spared the bloodshed and butchery suffered by the sacrificial lambs in their charge."

Kurt replied, "Yeah, and all the Nazi propaganda back home is wearing a little thin. But one thing is sure, my friend: the powerful Russian war machine will soon be at our very doorsteps, and I shudder to think what will become of our women and children."

Arie glanced over at the beardless raw recruits and asked, "Tell me, Kurt, should Ivan pay another call like this morning, how many of these mama's boys do you see surviving the day?"

"I wouldn't worry about them," Kurt answered. "I've never yet seen a new recruit who couldn't run faster scared than Ivan can mad. Quite frankly, I see the whole line collapsing if the Russkies come back anytime soon."

Twenty-six kilometers to the train station on a splendid summer day that was not half over—a very bearable distance for men hardened by months of forced marches in intolerable weather. Then an evening departure to the Fatherland. What motivation! With ten days of rest and relaxation to look forward to, they realized there was more to life after all than mere survival. Oh, how they longed to be free of this Russian purgatory!

It was the dog days of August, and the sun was altogether merciless. The men marched effortlessly over a flat stretch of dusty road with mere patches of birch and fir to break the monotony.

Farther on, Kurt gazed in awe at the opulent orchards and tall, sweeping crops lying in readiness for the fall harvest. Primitive wooden huts with sod roofs, tumbledown farm buildings, and occasional tree stands dotted the engaging landscape, which was surrounded on three sides by gently rolling hills. Along the western horizon before them lay a majestic mountain range marking the Rumanian frontier.

Kurt glanced over his shoulder to observe that the Front was little more than an insignificant streak on the horizon. His face broke into a wide smile. The odds in this pitiful game of life and death were stacked against the soldier ever reaching veteran status, but he and his best friend had found a way to cheat the system for better than three years.

"I can hardly believe it," Kurt remarked, a look of rapture upon his face. "We're free at last. We're on our way home!"

"I'll believe it when I'm strolling up the road to my mother's home and I sniff the scent of fresh bread drifting out her kitchen window," Arie declared in an incurably sad voice. "We've known so many setbacks. I dare not take anything for granted." Reaching for the Iron Cross dangling from his neck, he said, "You know, I'd swap this confounded trinket they awarded me to some high-stepping, egotistical Nazi officer for an extra week at home."

"I hear you. I've got nothing more glorious on my mind than sleep and letting my family spoil me rotten," Kurt remarked, allowing his invigorated imagination to carry him afar to the warm, cozy bed he last slept in during his previous furlough over a year ago.

Arie said, "You really must come down and call on me when this stinking mess is over. My mother is an exceptional cook, and you haven't lived until you've spent some time in the Bavarian Alps."

"Count on it, my friend," Kurt responded, patting him on the shoulder. "There are so many things I want to do when this sorry conflict has run its course that I only worry I won't have time for them all. But you can rest assured that visiting you is something I won't be denied."

Arie reached for the schnapps in his backpack, uncorked it, and tossed back a mighty swallow. His mother had been widowed for going on ten years, his father having done himself in with a hunting rifle to cut short a life marred by financial ruin and a debilitating bout of polio. Arie had suffered a miserable childhood as a result, and he habitually grappled with depression, even under the best of circumstances. On the Front, those were few and far between.

Kurt had come to appreciate his own upbringing, which was quite unlike Arie's background of adversity. His father was a tower of strength and a man to look up to: strong yet sympathetic, firm yet loving, honest, dependable, respected, and well liked in the community. He was the kind of man who'd go out of his way to help not only a friend or neighbor but also a total stranger. Kurt's mother was simply everything a good mother should be and much more. She was loving and thoughtful, committed to her family and to the values she held so dear. Kurt's enlistment had stolen some of the smile from her sweet, anxious face, but she clung to the hope that one day she'd again hold him in her arms.

Ahead on the roadside stood a German helmet suspended on the butt of a rifle that was stuck into the cold, black earth. Just another poor soul who would not be returning to his mother. Neither Kurt nor Arie broached the subject of death or serious injury, even though these misfortunes were so close at hand virtually every single day of their sorrowful journeys across Russia. They were painfully aware that their fragile existences could end in an instant at the mere whim of some stargazing officer aspiring to achieve personal recognition.

His tangled blond hair bouncing in the light summer breeze, Arie smiled and asked, "Your mother got some little heifer picked out for you in that little no-name town of yours? Or are you still stuck on that little honey back in Cologne?"

Kurt smiled to recall his one and only serious infatuation, which he had shared with Arie during their first month of basic training. Six months before enlisting, while attending a close friend's wedding in Cologne, Kurt had met a striking young lady with comely features and hair of gold. Her name was Marlene

Knappe. Visiting her in the company of friends after the wedding, he experienced something so intensely exhilarating that he doubted he could ever recapture it. "I don't think I'll ever get her off my mind," he told Arie. "I've tried to convince myself it was really her bubbly and spirited personality that stirred me, but ultimately it came down to the less honorable reality of her hard, firm body and striking beauty."

Arie laughed. "Hey, stop beating yourself up. What's to be expected of a seventeen-year-old?"

"I don't think I've ever told you this," said Kurt, "but, honest to God, I experienced this blissful, dizzying sensation that left me light-headed. Life took on a whole new meaning. I even lost my appetite. For days afterward, even sleep became a burden, like the chores and textbooks that plagued my adolescence."

"And you let her get away to some flyboy," Arie remarked.

"Yeah, that lucky guy's got her now, and so ends my lone venture into the realm of romance. How about you? Any ducks on the pond back in your neck of the woods?"

Arie slapped his buddy on the shoulder and replied with a smirk. "Hah. You, my friend, can have all the skirts in Germany. All I care about is getting back home, away from this madness." Laughing aloud, he added, "How about we change the subject to something less frustrating?"

As the sweeping grain fields gave way to a rugged, partially forested terrain, Kurt called for a ten-minute rest. Their weapons and backpacks were downright burdensome in the midday sun. Kurt swung his rifle off of his shoulder and collapsed to the earth with great satisfaction.

Recapturing an element of their squandered youth, they laughed aloud at even the most ridiculous efforts at humor.

Arie lustily kicked back a mouthful of schnapps with nary a twitch, passed the bottle to Kurt, and quipped, "What's the shortest book in the world? The Italian Book of War Heroes."

Shielding an extravagant yawn with the back of his hand, Kurt broke a generous smile, though he'd heard that one a time or two.

Arie lit a smoke and broke wind as only Arie could, a resounding detonation to shatter the hot, still air.

"Oh, cripes. Put a cork in it, will ya!" moaned Kurt, twisting his entire face into a knot and dragging his pack to a safer location. Arie looked on with the grinny, wide-mouthed satisfaction of a new bride.

Kurt lay back on the soft grass. "You should have heard Eckhart going on about Propaganda Minister Goebbels and our secret weapons. Our top scientists are at work on rockets and missiles that will be the end of the enemy once and for all," he chirped, his eyes ballooning with sarcasm. "These fatherless Commies will get what they've got coming, and then the backstabbing Brits and Yanks too."

Arie laughed. He had tossed his left boot and sock to one side to perform minor surgery on an irritating toenail. "Pinheaded Hitler Youth. That brain-dead kid's full of beans, but I'd give my left nut to see his dreams come true. My brother manning the antiaircraft over Cologne says the bombing has increased dreadfully in recent months, and the Western Allies are nearly at the Rhine."

Kurt nodded. "And did you hear Eckhart going on about our *Führer* the other night? I think he actually believes Hitler is going to pull this thing off yet."

"When everyone else has long given up on our besieged *Führer,* our naïve little buddy Eckhart will be there for him with a gleam in his eye and a touch of brown on his nose. Truth is, our *Führer* is a demented old fool," snapped Arie, drawing one last heavy drag before crushing out his cigarette. "My rear end knows more about snipe shooting than that imbecile does about running a war. We are doomed to defeat and can only hope that the Americans and British can beat the Russkies to Berlin."

Kurt appreciated Arie's frank evaluation of the crisis. Commentary of this type back at the Front —particularly Arie's potshot at the sacred cow himself—could bring about severe discipline, if not a firing squad. But on this untroubled stretch of road, one felt a certain boldness to express oneself openly.

"Eckhart thinks I'm a defeatist," said Arie. "I tell you I'm a realist through and through. I've spent the last three years killing Russians, and I'll spend another three years killing Russians if it means keeping them out of my country and away from my family. Unlike Eckhart, I have nothing personal against these poor devils. They're fighting for their very lives, and their homes, and their loved ones— just like you and me. We're like two fighting cocks in a pit, Ivan and me, neither one choosing to be there but both knowing his survival depends on ripping the other's heart out. What Eckhart needs is to get his head out from between his legs long enough to see what's going on in the real world."

Kurt bowed his head and ran his fingers through his hair. "It seems like such an immense waste to have fought this long and hard only to lose everything in the end."

"Yes," Arie answered. "I've tried to convince myself there may be some hope of reorganizing at our borders and holding back the invaders, but it's only wishful thinking."

CHAPTER FIVE

Back up on their feet, Kurt and Arie were jolted by gunfire and a distant explosion. They instinctively reached for their weapons, scanning the forested landscape for a clue to the conflict neither wanted anything to do with.

"Cursed partisans!" muttered Arie, turning to catch Kurt's reaction to the persistent woodland fire.

Kurt returned a puzzled look. An intense foreboding gripped him as he pondered his response. They were en route to the train terminal that would deliver them to a well-deserved and long-awaited sabbatical from the perdition of the Russian Front. A short distance away a battle was raging, doubtless involving German soldiers possibly in need of assistance. He gnawed his lower lip as his mind waged war with his heart.

"Let's go," ordered Kurt, breaking into a sprint.

"Go where?" Arie responded. "This isn't our fight."

"That intersection ahead. We're no more than a kilo from that gunfire. Someone may need our help, Arie." As Arie surged forward to join him, Kurt muttered a mostly silent prayer. "God, end it before we get there so we can be on our way to the station."

They achieved the intersection and dashed down a dilapidated road heading north, with no appreciable letup in the gunfire.

"Kurt, this is crazy!" yelled Arie. "We're on leave. We have no business here."

Gunfire rang in Kurt's ears as he contemplated renouncing the mission. His legs grew weary, and his lungs felt as though they would burst from the forced run. The road doglegged hard right, and it was there that they were able to assess the battle that he had prayed would be decided by now. Pausing to catch his breath and determine a course of action, he remembered a scene from a grade school picture book depicting American Indians circling a wagon train of settlers in the untamed West. A small German convoy had been ambushed and cut off from retreat by a band of bloodthirsty Soviet partisans who were now closing in for the deathblow.

Kurt turned to Arie. "Come in around the guerrillas on the left. I'll do the same on the right."

Arie complied, and they achieved complete surprise, raking the rebels with devastating fire.

A partisan who suddenly appeared from behind a large fir squeezed off two shots. Kurt reciprocated on the run, and his bullets smashed into the trunk, causing his assailant to duck behind the tree. As the partisan whirled and leaned out from the other side, Kurt released a concentrated volley, striking him dead center and sending him sprawling. His arms and legs twitched, and then his chest heaved in one final, hopeless gasp.

The insurgents broke rank and bolted deep into the woods in utter abandon. Unlike the morning's life-and-death battle with disciplined Russian soldiers, there were no pockets of defiance. Decidedly beaten, the partisans left only their dead to the bloodied battleground.

Kurt and Arie cautiously made their way to the road.

Amid the carnage that was once a modest German convoy stood an impressive SS officer, virtually unshaken by the gut-wrenching, life-threatening events. He flaunted a haughty countenance common to the disdained SS. Each member of this abhorrent branch of the armed forces had sworn personal loyalty and blind obedience to Hitler and his vile commands—no matter how decidedly deviant and demented any given directive may be. Brutal fanatics, moral degenerates—that was the norm. SS men considered themselves on a holy crusade to rid Eastern Europe of its Communist plague and inferior races.

These elite SS anti-partisan units were notorious for their savagery toward the rebels and the civilian populations that harbored them. In one nearby village, two thousand innocent inhabitants, primarily women and children, were put to death in retaliation for a partisan attack in the region. The goal of these sadistic units was to search out and destroy anyone suspected of defiance or of aiding the terrorist cause, and the SS increasingly employed those in the regular forces to assist with the dirty work.

For their part, the partisans seemed wholly intent on upping the SS ante in unconditional ruthlessness, slaughtering as many Germans as they could in as many horrific ways as possible. Though Kurt cursed and detested them for their dastardly hit-and-run tactics and barbaric means, deep down he possessed a grudging admiration.

At the officer's side was a ratty, dark-complexioned Russian with narrow, squinting eyes, a long straight nose, a grayish black beard, and a pitch-black matted mop parted straight down the middle. An informant or translator, he was in good favor with the officer and was most fortunate to have not fallen captive to the vindictive partisans.

The SS captain was noticeably short in stature, athletic, and well tanned. A pair of bushy eyebrows encased dark eyes set deeply into an uncommonly petite face, the right cheek of which featured an unsightly scar the length of his index finger. As Kurt strode toward him, the captain removed his cap to sweep back a strand of greasy, jet-black hair. Though inwardly pleased with Kurt, he deliberately braked short of a smile, which would be all too unbecoming a man of his disposition. With an unmistakable air of superiority, he asked, "Your name?"

"Corporal Kurt Muller, sir. Fifteenth Regiment of the Eighty-eighth Division, at your service," Kurt responded, saluting to feign respect for this man and his genocidal segment of the armed forces that Kurt had come to loathe.

"Captain Gerd Rykert," he returned, repaying the salute and extending his hand to shake Kurt's. "It appears we owe our lives to you, Corporal Muller. By the sweat on your brow, you seem to have been hard-pressed to immerse yourself in our little affair here."

Kurt pointed back over his shoulder. "We heard the shooting from the main highway, Captain. We were en route to the train station at Bessarabka to commence our leave," he continued, reaching into his pocket for the furlough papers and handing them to the officer.

"A well-deserved leave, I am sure, Muller," he remarked, scarcely perusing the documents before returning them. "And I am further assured that I won't be denied seeing to it that you receive a proper recognition, perhaps even the Iron Cross, for your heroics here today. Many a man would have passed us by, but you kindly suspended your journey to be the Good Samaritan."

"I was simply performing my duty, Captain. If a man is to be decorated for merely doing what he has been trained to do, then Germany must have an abundance of heroes, sir."

"Please, don't make light of your actions, Corporal. If the military had more men like you who would forsake the easy road for what will try them and make them hard, we would be having this conversation in a bathhouse in Moscow itself. You men are SS quality, Muller—perhaps even officer material. Maybe we can do something about that in the days to come. Now, you must excuse me while I attend to my men."

Kurt saluted as he departed, hoping their paths would never cross again.

Pickets stood guard while Kurt and Arie helped bury the SS dead in ridiculously shallow graves. Three of the injured were loaded into the captain's staff car. Another of the SS was instructed to drive the group back to headquarters after a blown front tire had been tended to.

As they departed, Rykert let slip a smile when addressing Kurt and Arie. "We'll gladly offer you men a ride to the train station, but I regret we must all squeeze into the personnel carrier. It's all we have left. We must first, however, complete our mission up the road." Assessing the disappointment on Kurt and Arie's faces, he added, "Cheer up, men. I can see you're not thrilled about it, but we simply must honor our brave comrades whom we've just laid to rest."

Kurt and Arie were exhausted and scarcely in humor for battle, but at least Rykert had guaranteed them a free ride to their destination upon completing the mission.

CHAPTER SIX

As they wound their way along the forested country road, Kurt tried to calm his battle-worn mind with thoughts of delightful days to come with his beloved family. His heart warmed at the prospect of joyful fellowship with his loved ones, delectable home cooking, unhindered sleep, and a blessed rest from the agonies of the Front. Peace, joy, and contentment—these were concepts alien to a man so caught up in the fiendish grip of war that he had all but forgotten their meaning, let alone how they might feel.

Kurt reflected on his youthful squad huddled beneath the intense Soviet cannonade. One dead, one wounded, and one subject to arrest—and the worst was still to come.

Kurt and Arie found themselves in the forced fellowship of three black-shirted SS: the implacable Captain Rykert; a brawny, black-eyed, boxer-nosed sergeant of evident ill humor; and a weedy, bespectacled private at the wheel of a well-weathered armored car rusted to the bone, its windshield cracked in a dozen places.

Kurt was on constant guard for partisans, his eagle eyes darting fretfully while his overactive imagination kept busy concocting a dozen gruesome scenarios. Arie manned the heavy machine gun atop the car, dutifully studying the rutted road for signs of the dreaded partisan land mines.

A gentle August breeze caressed the majestic pine trees lining the roadway, a scene so tranquil and diametrically opposed to that of the Front as to raise Kurt's hopes for a better tomorrow. A princely buck bolted across their path and faded into the welcoming forest. How Kurt envied it—for its God-blessed liberty to come and go as it pleased, unshackled by the burdensome cares and concerns of its own kind. Oh, that his own life could be so simple!

Kurt made a belated entry in his memoirs, recounting the episode with the guerrillas and their press-gang treatment by the SS. He planned to compile and publish his writings depicting his painful ordeal in an effort to influence others to do all in their power to prevent such a catastrophe from ever happening again. But how arrogant and presumptuous it was to think that he could have a hand in turning back the irresistible tide of human degradation! He was but a flyspeck drifting aimlessly in a cold, cruel world. Like millions of other unfortunates in his woebegone era, he had absolutely no choice in this hopeless venture. Rather, it was ungraciously thrust upon him like some malignant cancer.

He hoped to return one day to his homeland, no matter what its fate, where he would attempt to put in place the pieces of his shattered existence. He would once again feel the warmth and security of a real bed in a comfortable home and would taste flavorful and satisfying food. He would carry on with his life totally at peace with God and his world. He would endeavor to never again gripe about the weather or the economy or any other trivialities that, incredibly, once seemed significant. He hoped never again to shed the blood of his fellow man.

As for a future vocation, he dared not fulfill his boyhood aspiration to follow his grandfather into the ministry; his once virginal hands were much too defiled and his inward spirit much too seared to give thought to such a holy calling. He was but a whispery shadow of the self-respecting, vibrant young man who could lick his weight in wildcats and tackle any challenge, great or small. Kurt felt as though the war had transformed him into a thoughtless and uncaring killing machine, expertly programmed in acts of savagery but rendered physically spent, mentally battered, emotionally capsized, spiritually withered, and psychologically dispirited.

Like every mother's son wearing the uniform, he had become wholly disillusioned and heartsick over their army's continued presence in Russia. He could count only on his innate drive to survive to see him through to happier days. The joyous revelry succeeding their effortless conquest of France—when they carried on as though the war was won—seemed light years away. The *Führer*'s enigmatic decision to invade Russia in a quest for "living space" for the "superior" German people had led to Germany's complete downfall. The entire nation would be called to account for his mindless delusion.

Kurt could see nothing of value in this cheerless ordeal. He despised this disgusting war and every single thing to do with it, beginning with the ten months of basic training. That had been nothing less than a designed, deliberate dehumanization of impressionable young men who had been brought up otherwise. They had taught him how to hate and how to kill. Nothing else mattered. But then Nazism itself was begotten of hatred and nurtured by violence, and sadly the German people had bought into it unreservedly, often zealously. They would live to reap the horrifying harvest of an exceptionally bad seed.

His reflective melancholy was suspended by the captain. "Would you say you enjoy life in the military, Muller?" he questioned, drawing heavily on a cigar as they bounced along the potholed and sullied trail.

"To be honest, Captain, I'm sick and tired of this bloody war and would give anything to be free from it all and go home for good."

"So, you're saying you'd rather not be here fighting for your country?"

"I love my country, sir, and I will do my duty, no matter the personal cost."

"That's fair enough," Rykert remarked, exchanging his somber demeanor for one much lighter and less intimidating. He leaned back and recoiled into a winsome smile. "To be sure, most men would give anything for an end to this war. Not me. I love it—the war and all the death and human heartache that come with it." He inhaled deeply, then exhaled the smoke through his mouth and nose. "Do you find that hard to believe, Muller?"

"No, sir, I can't say that I do. They say that one man's meat is another man's poison. In the same way that a fire cannot survive without oxygen, war must have its warmongers. I'm happy that you have found your niche, Captain. It's not often one meets someone so at peace with himself out here."

"You don't approve," he glowered, his eyes mere slits.

"It is not up to me to approve or disapprove, Captain. My duty is to follow orders and trust in those with authority over me to make the right decisions," Kurt answered, voicing the standard expectation of the enlisted man as best as he could remember it from basic training.

Rykert's cigar became a pointer. "Muller, I sense something missing deep inside. You know what you need? A vision. A cause. A purpose for living. A commitment to something worthwhile. And maybe you'll just stumble upon it in that little village up ahead."

The informant spoke to Rykert, and Kurt was offered a reprieve. The dialogue brought back a hurtful recollection from his boyhood of handsomely attired men riding in headlong pursuit of a thoroughly terrified, resplendent red fox. As his father and he witnessed from their horse-drawn plough, shots rang out. The disabled creature toppled gracelessly, struggled to regain its balance, then wobbled along, striving to elude its assailants, a victim of man's blood lust. A subsequent discharge blew apart its head, the jubilant hunters encircling their prey with extreme satisfaction before riding off and leaving it to rot in the meadow.

Kurt's heart had sunk in sorrow over the unjust end of this magnificent little creature, and he had asked, "Why did they kill the fox, Father?"

"Killing is a sport to some men," his father replied. "They do it for the sheer enjoyment of taking a life. You might say they kill simply for the sake of killing."

Kurt was slapped back to attention as their dust-drenched journey came to an end. Little did he know his life was about to be turned upside down. A fatal fall-out from the often-conflicting calls to duty and honor raced toward him with the speed and fury of God's avenging angels.

Arie addressed the officer. "Captain Rykert, there's a small hamlet through the clearing ahead, sir."

The informant came alive, blathering on like a man gone mad.

"Drive straight on in," Rykert ordered, seemingly unmindful of enemy action in the sleepy, unassuming little village.

They stopped at a sizable outbuilding on the periphery. The captain had the look of someone who had just stumbled upon a gold mine. "Encircle the entrance," he barked.

The adrenaline flowed freely as the men carried out the order. Arie was left out in front of the barn with his machine gun riveted on the entry. Rykert, the sergeant, and the informant strode confidently toward the door and swung it open, again strangely oblivious to danger.

Kurt marveled at the death-defying nerve—or was it the carelessness—of these men in confronting a nest of desperate insurgents in this fashion.

The informant screamed a call to surrender and seconds later repeated his summons. Shadowy shapes emerged from a trap door of what appeared to be a basement hideout.

CHAPTER SEVEN

Kurt sighed at the prospect of avoiding a deadly gun battle as more of the hapless foe appeared. The captain was right—just a slight detour and then on to the train station for their joyous journey home.

Shielding their eyes from the sun's blinding brightness, the forlorn figures filed out into the open.

It was then that Kurt and Arie realized with utmost revulsion what the captain's mission was about. These were not partisans but Jews, clearly evident from their characteristic clothing and hairstyles. Men, women, and children emerged, some openly distressed, others compliantly conceding their fate, every last one understanding that their day of reckoning with the dreaded, death-dealing SS had come.

Arie and Kurt had witnessed the bewildering and repulsive slaughter of Jews by the SS or their equally repugnant SD counterparts, and either one had absolutely no stomach for it. For this "mission," they had buried four SS.

His face pinched tight, Arie called out Kurt's name in a most unsteady voice.

Kurt turned to behold a thoroughly distressed Arie gawking at him with pleading eyes, the color fading from his countenance as they spoke, his finger wrapped around the trigger of the weapon they both understood would be the one chosen for the grisly execution to come.

"They're Jews. I want no part of this, do you hear?"

"I hear you, Arie," Kurt answered. "I want no part of this either, I assure you."

The Jews were assembled outside the barn, and Rykert set the seasoned structure aflame with the aid of a canister of petrol.

Kurt's troubled gaze fixed upon a tearful little girl of no more than seven with the face of a lamb who shook as with a bout of pneumonia. Standing in the midst of the woe-inspiring pack and whimpering aloud, she clutched a tattered doll in one arm and cleaved despondently to her thoroughly distraught mother with the other, the embodiment of outright despair.

Although she spoke in a tongue foreign to him, Kurt fully understood the little girl's meaning as she asked, "Why, Mommy? What have we done wrong?"

Her mother knelt to take the little girl in her arms, striving to offer words of reassurance, but there were none to offer. They would die that day. And for what reason? She herself couldn't understand why, let alone explain it.

Suddenly, a young boy broke for the woodland. A woman lunged at the nearby SS sergeant to cover his flight. Coolly, the sergeant brushed her aside, drew and engaged his machine pistol, riddling the audacious youngster with a fatal burst. Her eyes transfixed with horror, the woman raved in anguish and struggled with her tormentor, only to be shot in the head by the unmerciful Rykert, thus ending the condemned prisoners' sole effort to regain their priceless liberty.

The others were like sheep before the shearer, powerless to alter the crushing course of events pressing down upon them, presumably resigned to their death sentence as though it were somehow just and understandable.

As the stone-hearted Rykert and his sergeant approached him, Kurt's lips moved in prayer that he would be spared a role in this barbaric act. He felt overwhelmed by a sudden onslaught of shock and nausea. How much more of this heartless insanity could he withstand before being shipped home to his parents in the fetal position, diapered and sucking his thumb?

"Corporal, you may direct your man to open fire on this pestilence," instructed Rykert, motioning with a thumb. "The sooner we get it done, the sooner we have you at the train station." He gently gripped Kurt's arm as he passed, as though imparting a pardon for his role in this immoral undertaking.

Kurt broke into a cold sweat, the blood draining from his face, his legs all but failing him as he stood beneath enormous pressure. He gazed confoundedly upon the condemned, their faces miserable masks of terror.

With the barn fully ablaze behind them, the captives turned to embrace friends and family; some dropped to their knees, and others openly wailed in distress. Kurt's eyes fell upon a young family of four huddled together in a circle and alternately praying and singing to their God. He recalled how his own family would sing and pray together in a more favorable time blessedly undisturbed by war and its accompanying condemnable insensitivity.

For the unfeeling SS, this was just another run-of-the-mill village, just one more expendable band of repulsive Jews. Living monuments to man's inhumanity, the SS had long since given themselves over to psychopathic, cold-blooded murder, mandated by the almighty Hitler himself to carry out the wholesale eradication of Jews, gypsies, and other "unacceptables". So grandly commissioned, they considered themselves on an entirely principled and legitimate crusade about which they need feel neither responsibility nor shame.

This concept of forced obligation and the resulting ethical exoneration swept over Kurt like a cool breeze, relieving the piercing pain of conscience, as he realized it was not his to question why. Rather, he must at all costs be true to his military oath and so submit to whatever orders were assigned him, regardless of his personal convictions. Hadn't thousands of fellow servicemen taken part in similar executions these past years? Could he in any way be held morally responsible for the deaths of these poor souls, no matter how unmistakably unjust or blatantly unethical? He was a soldier, and his sworn duty was to obey orders, even when they flowed contrary to his perception of honor and morality.

Then he looked again upon the woeful, grief-stricken individuals assembled before him. All his self-serving rationalizations vanished with the wind. He could scarcely imagine the insufferable agony being played out before his eyes as the captives waited in their innocence for a callous command to bring on a death ordinarily reserved for society's vilest offenders.

Caught on the horns of a decidedly diabolic dilemma, scrambled thoughts raced like a runaway train through Kurt's embattled conscience, inducing a nerve-shattering panic. His impassioned sense of self-preservation lashed him relentlessly, like an infuriated flood tide at the beleaguered pillars of his moral foundation.

"Corporal," came a wintry voice from behind, a scowling and growling Rykert communicating his displeasure at Kurt's hesitation to deliver the devilish command.

Yet Kurt remained paralyzed in indecision as searing deliberations burned away in his brain. As a dutiful soldier, he was compelled to carry out the gruesome command; as an honorable, God-fearing human being, however, he was every bit as much compelled to refuse to do so. So he waited, helpless to act and expecting at any moment to be placed under guard or, more likely, thrown up against a wall and shot.

His wait was not prolonged. The SS sergeant stepped over and administered a malicious blow to the side of his head that sent him reeling to the ground, helmet sailing through the air. "Give the order, you insubordinate swine!" he bellowed, fixing Kurt angrily, training his pistol squarely at his head.

Kurt stared incredulously, first at the sergeant and then at Rykert, the lump in his throat rivaling the knot in the pit of his stomach. "We're not SS butchers. We're German soldiers!" he raged, struggling to keep his voice from cracking under the unabated strain. "This is not our concern!"

Kurt perceived that it was now the end for him; better he had fallen gloriously at the front like Zillstra or a thousand like him. He felt entirely embittered and betrayed. How could his country—certainly one of the most highly developed in the world—have sunk to such a depth?

What seemed like whole minutes but were actually mere seconds elapsed. He lay helpless on the ground, clutching his rifle and frantically searching his muddled mind for an answer only his hurting heart could provide to deal with the cruel dilemma bearing down on him.

The sergeant petitioned his captain for the charge to execute him. Yet, to Kurt's astonishment, he was spared.

"You disappoint me, Muller," pronounced the captain. "I truly envisioned you as SS material, but I see you simply haven't the nerve. I really should have let Sergeant Stein put an end to you, but you did save my life today. Now get up and stand out of the way, and let the real men do their duty." He turned to Arie with a wintry gaze. "Begin firing, Private!"

As Kurt gained his feet, Arie faced him once again, looking for his endorsement to proceed with the execution. "Kurt?" he implored.

Kurt observed a heavy bead of sweat drip from Arie's chin as the escalating anguish took its toll. Able to empathize with his subordinate, a vexing perception of guilt came over him. He realized that his own reluctance had merely relegated responsibility for this atrocity to Arie. Yet, he recognized further that he dared not grant his approval to yield to the command or defy it.

The sergeant directed his pistol at Arie and looked to Rykert for approval.

An image of dark, profound depravity, the captain raised his voice. "Open fire, Private. This is my final warning."

Kurt looked caringly into Arie's storm-tossed eyes. Arie too had become arrested by conscience and would perish for his compassionate stand. When Arie placed his shaking hands upon the machine gun to muster enough conviction to carry out the brutal decree, Kurt realized that, after all, Arie might lower himself to commit the odious offense out of sheer self-preservation—a ghastly occurrence he dared not allow.

Rykert turned to his subordinate, about to deliver the order for Arie's execution, when, as if by reflex in a completely irrational moment of decision, Kurt raised his rifle and uttered his own ultimatum, his voice again on the brink of splintering: "Drop the weapon, Sergeant."

The sergeant turned only briefly to consider Kurt's audacious command before refocusing on Arie.

Kurt softened his voice. "I'm telling you to stand down, soldier, or I'll end your sorry existence right here and now."

Rykert stepped closer, his eyes tightened in disbelief, his tone a blend of confusion and irritation. "Have you lost your mind, Corporal? Too long in the trenches?" He gestured toward the Jews. "You're putting your life on the line for this heap of human trash?"

Kurt turned his weapon upon the captain to check his advance. "Arie and I want nothing to do with this inhumane slaughter of yours, that's all. I made that clear to you, but you refused to listen. And now it's come to this."

"Fine...fine, Corporal Muller. Just lower your firearm and step away. Sergeant Stein will jump up and take over the machine gun. All right?" Rykert turned to his subordinate. "Sergeant."

Arie gladly relinquished his post, grabbed his rifle, and leapt to the ground.

Stein holstered his pistol and stepped up to the machine gun.

Rykert issued the order without taking his eyes off Kurt. "Fire when ready, Sergeant."

"No, stop!" Kurt yelled. "Get down from there, or I swear I'll blow your head off."

Rykert took on a devilish sneer. "Oh, so I see this has little to do with you and your friend here. You've taken a liking to our captives."

As Kurt turned his attention to the captain, the sergeant swung into action, reaching for the pistol at his side.

Kurt responded instinctively. Turning and embracing his Mauser, he shot his assailant dead in the chest, dispatching the contemptible creature headlong to the earth.

Desperate glances were exchanged haphazardly among the bug-eyed SS commander, Kurt, and Arie. Years of unearthly brutal war on the Eastern Front could not possibly have prepared them for this. Dumbfounded, they waited for the next card to fall. For his part, Kurt felt a deepening hue of shame. He ogled the stone-dead SS sergeant with shock and penitence.

The SS driver, who'd been sent to check the village for more Jews, reappeared on Kurt's blind side. Realizing an insurrection was in progress, he leveled his rifle at Kurt. Suddenly a shot rang out, and Kurt whirled around to see the man collapsing to the earth, discharging his firearm skyward in the process. Arie had joined the insurrection by delivering Kurt from a bullet to the back.

The relief on the faces of the condemned Jews was evident as they witnessed the incident in total disbelief. Were they to be spared?

"Drop your weapons!" trumpeted the blue-faced Rykert, his right index finger extended, his fearful focus shifting from Arie to Kurt. Panicky glances were bandied about, followed by the captain reaching for his holstered Luger.

As Kurt caught a glimpse of the Russian snitch vanishing into the compacted growth of trees to his right, he felt the blistering heat of Rykert's damning glare. He realized that his life would never be the same. Kurt trained his rifle on Rykert, prompting him to leave his weapon in place. "That's enough!" Kurt yelled, slowly repossessing a measure of his splintered composure. "There's been too much senseless slaughter on this mission of yours already, Captain. No more! You could have left us out of this."

A growing insecurity had robbed Rykert of his bluster. "You men will live to regret this day. You've damned yourselves to hell for the sake of these subhumans." Discerning that he had no more cards to play, he backed toward the armored car.

"Stop," yelled Kurt.

Rykert slid into the driver's seat. "Are you going to shoot me, Corporal? In cold blood? I think not. Or have you some notion to bind my hands and take me along with you? I'd sooner be dead. Do what you must."

"Rykert!" screamed Kurt as the officer engaged the ignition. "I'll make you a deal. You drive off safe and sound in exchange for leaving us alone here."

"I don't make deals with scum-of-the-earth traitors, and frankly I don't think you have the stomach to carry through with your threat." With a finger pointed menacingly in Kurt's direction, he engaged the gear shift and growled, "I will be back for you two Jew-lovers, and I'll track you to the gates of hell. You'll pay for your treachery. Now, you will grant my men a proper burial before launching your hopeless flight, won't you?"

Despite the manifest sobriety of the hour, Kurt got in a parting shot laced with sarcasm. "I imagine this has put a bit of a damper on that Iron Cross you talked about?"

Rykert's words came through clenched teeth. "You possess a remarkable sense of humor for a condemned man, Corporal. Do enjoy your freedom while it lasts. We will meet again, and I guarantee you won't be so unmannerly when we do."

The Jews embraced one another and wept out loud as the promise of their deliverance dawned on them.

As Rykert started off, Kurt was joined by Arie. His brow deeply furrowed with a grave expression of resolve, he elevated his rifle at the departing vehicle.

"We're no better than he is if you pull that trigger, Arie. We can't allow him to drag us down to his disgusting level," Kurt said, gripping the weapon and lowering it. "We killed these SS men in self-defense. What you are contemplating is out-and-out murder."

Jerking it from Kurt's grasp with gnashed teeth, Arie argued, "Murder...self-defense...I couldn't care less. I'm concerned only with surviving this war, and I know we have absolutely no chance with that sadistic animal running free."

Kurt recaptured his hold on the rifle, this time with both hands. "And the informant who made off through the trees; are you going to eliminate him too? Think about it, man. We're fugitives with or without Rykert, and we have to cling to every fragment of humanity this stinking war has left us. Now, let it go, Arie, I beg you."

CHAPTER EIGHT

His customary congeniality missing in action, Arie backed away. He began to fashion a shallow grave for the departed SS, while his great friend and comrade attempted to make sense of the impossible circumstance they had been cast into.

Kurt turned toward the Jews. He considered that they were most fortunate to be alive, if being alive in Russia in 1944 could be considered good fortune. A stunning, curvaceous young woman of natural, timeless beauty and a weathered, sun-browned and strongly built man of about fifty approached him.

"We are hopelessly indebted to you, Corporal, for having saved our lives," said the beautiful girl in flawless German. "May God bless your honorable stand here today. My name is Elena Brausma, and this man is our leader and my uncle, Micah Schechter. Unfortunately, he doesn't understand a word of German, so I must interpret for him."

While shaking Micah's hand and exchanging greetings, Kurt identified him as a kind and gentle and yet strong and spirited individual.

Kurt tipped his cap to the lady. "You speak perfect German, Miss," he observed, captivated by her lovely, rich brown eyes. Her shoulder-length raven-black hair highlighted her splendor, and the smooth, ravishing skin was to die for, but those eyes…

She replied, "I am German-born, but my parents thought it best to send me to stay with my uncle in 1938, just when things were becoming unbearable for Jews in Germany. They thought I would be safe from the Nazis here. Until today, they were quite right."

Stricken by her comeliness, Kurt was momentarily oblivious to his beastly predicament and stood silent before her. He wanted to speak but could not find the words.

Fortunately, the older gent snapped the awkwardness with a rambling Russian discourse; his sagacious old eyes commanded Kurt's immediate respect.

"My uncle wishes to extend his warmest thanksgiving on behalf of our people. He is concerned about what you will do now that you have acted against your officer. Will he not be back with more men? Won't that be bad for you?"

"Yes, he'll be back soon. And, to be sure, that will be exceedingly bad for all of us," Kurt responded. "As for you people, I can only wish you Godspeed in getting as far away from here as possible. That will be our task as well—to set off at once and hopefully reach the Rumanian border."

Elena conveyed Kurt's response to the Russian leader. He responded with a burst of speech, the tips of his mustache rippling with excitement.

Elena spoke again. "My uncle is extremely worried for you men. For us it is not difficult to locate another safe place. We've heard that the Russian army is close by and will soon liberate us. But for you there is no liberation. There is only danger everywhere: partisans, the Russian army, and now your own people. And food—what will you do for food?"

Kurt was impressed with the Jews' genuine regard for his and Arie's plight, but he was puzzled about what they thought they could possibly accomplish on his behalf. "I assure you, young lady, you need not feel bad nor in any way responsible for our predicament. You should concern yourself only with regaining a safe haven for yourselves. We are trained soldiers who have weathered far worse than this. We're quite able to fend for ourselves, thank you."

Elena's interpretation resulted in more gibberish from the old Russian, this time with a marked emotional character, his hands alive with gesture.

"My uncle would be honored to have you enter into hiding with us and await the Soviet liberators. He would take up your case with them and see that you receive the best of treatment until this dreadful war has passed."

Kurt smiled at their naïveté. "Please inform your uncle that we appreciate his proposal, but we would sooner take our chances with our own forces than fall into Russian captivity. We'll be all right if we can make it across the border. The Rumanians are fed up with the fighting."

As he withdrew from her company, he ached with an inner longing he'd never known. He wondered if he had in fact been in dialogue with one of God's own cherubs. He wished this war would let up just long enough to allow the luxury of resuming this blessed interlude.

The young lady translated Kurt's response to the old man's thoughtful invitation, which resulted in further electrified argument.

Contemplating his actions, Kurt pictured a fork in the road mapped by Captain Rykert under the guiding hand of Satan himself. Of the two pathways, he knew he had chosen well. He examined the haggard collection of souls before him. They were now charged with launching a new game of hide-and-seek with men driven by hate and given over to boundless cruelty. Had he to do over again, he would take whatever measures to save these people from execution, no matter the outcome.

Elena returned to him. "Begging your pardon, Corporal. My uncle has asked that I talk to you once more before we make our way. He would like to extend his services to you as a guide to assist in gaining your freedom. He knows every square kilometer of this territory and could help you forage for food and see you safely to your destination. And I would…I would be honored to come along as interpreter, if you will have me."

Overwhelmed by Micah's sensible proposal and thoroughly overjoyed with the opportunity to further his implausible fantasy with this gorgeous young lady, Kurt nodded his head.

Elena returned to her uncle, leaving Kurt to observe with deep satisfaction her wondrous, God-given form.

Kurt took notice of a sunken-chested, sandy-haired little boy, his handsome face and large, sunny blue eyes doused in tears, who was drifting unsteadily toward the beautiful girl. A portly elderly woman was in tow. The three of them approached Kurt. Elena spoke for them.

"Corporal, if we may have another moment of your time, this young fellow would like to present you with a token of gratitude for saving his life today. His parents were executed by the Nazis just over a year ago. He lived with his aunt and cousin, who were killed outside the barn today. He would like you to have this hand-carved whistle, which his cousin gave him just yesterday. It would mean a great deal to him."

Kurt accepted the gift; he knelt to thank the little boy. The boy was chock-full of fortitude even after witnessing the brutal slaying of his relatives—the people most capable of giving him purpose and meaning in this otherwise troublesome existence. Kurt's heart was wrung with pity. He lightly patted the youngster's tearstained cheek, shook his trembling little hand, and tenderly embraced him. More tears welled up in those big, blue eyes already sodden with sorrow, inducing a like response in Kurt's.

"Thank you…very much," Kurt said, pausing to regain his composure in the midst of the heartrending moment, one that he knew would remain forever etched in his memory. He awaited the translation into the boy's language and added, "I will keep it always and cherish it with all my heart."

Moved to tears by the boy's selfless offering, Kurt reached for the chain dangling about his neck—an invaluable memento from his parents following his enlistment—depicting Christ nailed to the cross. "I want you to have this," he said, pressing it into the boy's tiny hand. "You may not know the man in this picture, but he was a Jew, like you. He suffered many hardships similar to yours. I hope it will encourage you, the way it has me, to maintain your faith in all the hard times to come."

Subsequent to the translation, the child lifted his heavy, tear-filled eyes to meet Kurt's. *"Dyakooyoo,"* he responded in a gentle voice. Then he turned away with a disquieted smile to his loved ones' funeral.

Kurt slowly made his way over to where Arie was digging the graves. Mere hours ago these two were in the highest of spirits, prancing down a dusty highway, laughing aloud, carrying on like boys commencing summer vacation. Now they shared the look of those chained to the oars of a sinking slave ship.

Kurt said, "Arie, I am forever indebted to you for the stand you took today. I owe you my life. Back on the road to the station, I felt the need to go to the aid of men I've come to see weren't worthy of it. The only thing that matters is that we are now alone in this country with no friends, no allies. We must make a run for it. I'm truly sorry for the state we're in here, but we need one another now more than ever so that we can look forward to seeing our families again."

Arie reached to shake Kurt's hand. Though utterly awash in a black sea of self-pity, he could find no fault in his great friend. "We're up crap creek without a paddle, old buddy, but you have nothing to apologize for."

Kurt patted him on the shoulder and then withdrew to ponder their course of action. He sank to the earth with his legs folded beneath him, his head in one hand and his rifle in the other, wishing with all his heart he could make it all go away.

CHAPTER NINE

Micah made final preparations for the departure of his people, leaving them in the care of the village rabbi. He had convinced Kurt and Arie of an escape route to the Black Sea. From there, they could try to reach neutral Turkey by boat. A hat had been passed among Micah's people to secure Russian currency to purchase Kurt and Arie's freedom in the form of a boat ride, once they reached the Ukrainian coastal town of Tatarbunary.

Kurt recalled a passage from Ecclesiastes his grandfather had read to him as a boy: "Then I looked again at all the acts of oppression which were being done under the sun. And behold I saw the tears of the oppressed and that they had no one to comfort them; and on the side of their oppressors was power, but they had no one to comfort them. So I congratulated the dead who are already dead more than the living who are still living. But better off than both of them is the one who has never existed, who has never seen the evil activity that is done under the sun." Surely this prophesied the Russian Front. Kurt would have wished for the dead SS to rest in peace, if in fact they were deserving.

Arie took point as they began their run to the coast, and Micah joined him.

At this lowest point, Elena joined Kurt as they made for the shadowy forest ahead. So unaccustomed to the companionship of a pretty young lady, he scarcely knew how to conduct himself.

"May I walk with you for a while, Corporal?" she inquired.

"Only if you refrain from calling me by my rank. My name is Kurt, Kurt Muller. Where are you from?"

"From Hamburg."

"Hamburg! I'm from Bremen. We're practically neighbors, for goodness' sake! I'm indeed charmed to make your acquaintance, Elena, and I can't tell you how pleasant it is to talk to such a beautiful young woman this far from civilization."

She dissolved into a deep blush, a color that looked very good on her, and once again she favored Kurt with that expansive smile. "You may wonder at my saying it, Kurt, but I can easily empathize with you and your friend in what you are experiencing today. You see, I too had to run for my freedom in 1938, and I finished up hiding away like an animal in the cellar of that stable to avoid capture and extermination at the hands of people I once considered my own. My crime was having a Jewish mother, and I was sentenced to death, without trial and without reason. By refusing to carry out our execution, you also have had to abandon your country and go into hiding. We most certainly have a great deal in common."

"My abandonment is only temporary, I assure you of that, Elena. I'll go back to Germany one day with head held high. Reason and sanity will one day return to our country—or what's left of it when the Allies get through with us. You, too, will be an appreciated member of society there. You'll see."

She coerced a quick smile and responded in a weak voice. "I certainly hope so, but I can't help wondering about the fate of my parents and brothers back in Germany. I stopped receiving letters four months before your invasion of Russia, and I fear the worst. Those in our group have witnessed shootings and deportations of Jews by the hundreds. We've been most fortunate to have eluded the SS thus far."

"It's madness," Kurt replied. "Men like Rykert will pay for their villainy one day. You can count on it!" He started to reassure Elena as to the destiny of her family, but he quit in mid-sentence when he considered that they truly had scant prospect of survival, what with the treatment of Jews he had witnessed in Russia. Would Hitler, that lunatic, be any less exacting in his handling of this disdained race in his own backyard? So Kurt merely imparted his inmost sympathy and his desire for a favorable outcome and left it at that, regretting he had addressed the hopeless situation.

Kurt said, "I remember reading, as a child, a passage from the Bible in which God raises up all the rulers of this world for his own good purpose and then sets them down in his time. I've often wondered, then, what could possibly account for Hitler's rise to power. How could a God of inexpressible love and kindness even condone such an abomination, let alone be responsible for it?"

"I've wondered about that too. But I've found it most difficult to believe in a God these past years. My father is Catholic and my mother Jewish, so religion was a prime topic in our household. But why should God allow so much suffering?"

"Man's heart is evil. That's how I get around it. When men like Rykert shut out God's love and light, all hell breaks loose in this world."

She smiled. "You have a depth to you, Kurt Muller. I like that."

Although subjected to sweltering heat and humidity, the foursome reveled in nature's grandeur, their flickering faith flowering with every stride taken toward their cherished freedom. The heat was downright burdensome; their sleeves were rolled up past the elbows, their shirts sweat-stained nearly to the belt.

Presently, they passed a colossal Stalinist collective farm that teemed with human and animal activity. Nestled contentedly at the foot of gently rolling hills paneling the skyline, its inhabitants were clearly oblivious to the coming chaos a short distance to the east. At Kurt's feet, wildflowers and dandelions danced gaily in a seductive southerly breeze, while overhead a pair of love struck sparrows hovered playfully. With Micah and Arie in the lead, the renegade band climbed a succession of hills and wound their way through a valley and across a flourishing grain field before pausing to nibble at a sumptuous orchard.

Elena had no way of knowing the energy and zest for life she was implanting in Kurt's worn body, soul, and mind with her near-constant chatter, as they recommenced their passage and ploughed along without respite for better than three hours. Was God compensating him for his decision to act on behalf of these scapegoats of Hitler's unconscionable hate?

So enraptured by their delightful conversation was he that Kurt was actually disappointed—though his weary feet were in total agreement—when Micah announced a rest beside a fresh, tree-lined stream. Kurt sensed that he was falling in love with this elegant creature and would, in all likelihood, end up with a very large hole in his heart. The preceding hours at her side were an oasis in the otherwise desert-like social atmosphere of this land.

Arie and Micah joined Elena and Kurt beside the stream, and the foursome shared some of the provisions.

Elena extended her hand to Arie. "Arie, allow me to take the opportunity to thank you for your part in saving our lives at the village. I am forever indebted. It was very self-sacrificing, and I just know that some good is meant to come out of all this yet."

"Rykert didn't exactly leave us with any choice. I'd sooner have died there myself than be part of a senseless execution."

"Have you and Kurt known one another long?"

"Hmph…too long," Arie snorted, before throwing an arm around Kurt. "I almost feel like he's an appendage of some sort."

His heart warming at the sight of the two most significant people in his tossed-up world engaged in cordial conversation, Kurt said, "Did you know this inarticulate Bavarian was once my superior, a full sergeant major in our regiment?"

"A sergeant?" Elena responded respectfully with raised eyebrows.

"Yes, it's true," acknowledged Arie, a boyish smirk settling upon his face. "Until the night I rearranged the face of a military policeman in a barroom brawl in Dnepropetrovsk."

Elena crossed her arms and tightened her face. "Well, I'm sure he had it coming."

Kurt jumped in with marked sarcasm. "Arie was drunker than a brewer's fart. And, oh yes, that MP had it coming, all right. Can you imagine the nerve of that man calling Arie a clumsy young pig-dog? I mean, nobody calls Arie 'young' and gets away with it."

Arie laughed softly, a sheepish grin adorning his face. "It seems I've just got a thing for MPs. Whenever I see one of those pond scum, I want to reach out and commit a crime. You know what I mean? At any rate, our captain was none too delighted and very quick to relieve me of those stripes, but at least he spared me a trip to a punishment battalion."

"All joking aside, I owe my life to this man," Kurt stated, placing his hand on Arie's right shoulder. "Today wasn't the first time he saved my life."

"Tell me about it," she replied.

"It was in the spring of '42 during our capture of the Crimea that a leg wound nearly did me in. We were advancing on a concrete bunker, our guys falling left and right, when an explosion knocked me clean off my feet. I was barely conscious, and the pain in my thigh overwhelmed me. I howled like a man gone mad but was sure no one could possibly hear me above the noise of battle."

Arie interjected with a light laugh. "He was whimpering like a little baby, I swear."

Elena placed her hands on her hips and responded defensively, "Well, no doubt. I'm sure anybody else would have passed out completely and died of shock."

Kurt continued, "Well, I did in fact lose consciousness, slowly gliding away just as Arie came to my rescue. I should surely have died from blood loss or have been blown to kingdom come had my heroic sidekick here not carried me away to safety. It's a strange feeling—when you think you're dying. A helpless, hopeless feeling. Not a thing you can do about it. And then you come out of it. Strange, very strange. Fortunately, the cards fell in my favor. The shrapnel failed to find any bone or major arteries, and I was spared amputation."

Arie jumped in again. "Though they handled him with the care more appropriate to an animal than a human being, Kurt absolutely bathed the medics in gratitude upon his release some weeks afterward."

Elena placed her hand on Kurt's knee, smiling widely, "Always the gracious gentleman."

Kurt observed Elena performing the same magic with Arie she had with him, boosting his spirits through cordial conversation.

Elena and her uncle left to gather some wild berries, allowing Kurt and Arie a dip in the slow-moving stream. Tall reeds swayed gracefully. Mature trees, rimmed by adoring saplings, stood guard along the lush banks. Kurt and Arie happily scoured away weeks of dirt and grit from their neglected bodies.

"Do I detect a passing interest in that little Jewess?" Arie remarked with a grin.

"Heaven help me, Arie; I can't remember ever feeling this way about anyone. Does it show?"

"Just a bit," he answered, gently slapping Kurt on the shoulder. "Well, you can't be faulted on your taste. She's a honey."

"Am I just fooling myself here? I mean, what can I possibly hope to gain from this?" asked Kurt.

"What's it matter if you are fooling yourself? What have you got to lose? She's worth the investment, and it seems to be mutual. She's not exactly shying away from you."

"Yeah, but I keep expecting that uncle of hers to take after me with his belt."

Arie laughed and said, "You just keep your hands where they belong and no harm will come to you."

Arie had gone off to answer the call of nature, and Kurt was out of the water and nearly dressed when Elena emerged to hand him an apple, her soft hands lightly touching his. Kurt practically dissolved at her touch. And those eyes!

The sun was in full retreat but hadn't taken with it much of its warmth. Sitting side by side with their knees pulled up to their chests, Kurt shared some of his waning provisions along the embankment as they carried on in blissful dialogue.

"So, Kurt, what do you hope to do with yourself following the war?"

"Oh, I guess I don't much bother myself with great career plans or anything. My father has a farm—not a big farm, but he's done well by it—as did his father and grandfather before him. Unless something else comes along, I just see myself moving back there and fitting in again."

"That's marvelous. Farming is a very honorable occupation, and I'm sure you'll do very well at it."

"And how about you, Elena Brausma? Any plans once you get back home?"

Pausing to collect her thoughts and pawing nervously at the grass with the heel of her boot, she replied with a shake of her head, "I used to have such really incredible plans for my life. I'm just too embarrassed to share them with anybody."

"No, please do."

"Well, let's see." She smiled, tossing back her head and gazing dreamily at the heavens. "I'll only bore you with the most outstanding ones. Before the war, I had a very great interest in travel—world travel. I'd sit and dream about exotic lands and wish I had the wings of an eagle. I looked into Foreign Service opportunities, everything from nursing and teaching to office work in a German embassy. And I very much would have liked to be part of a world-renowned orchestra, touring the continent making music and meeting exciting people."

She paused with tears on the horizon, her bottom lip curling under as she wrung the very blood from her hands. "It seems so very strange now, but I was brought up to believe that this world was for the taking. And then the war came along, and I've spent the last few years dreaming about nothing more glorious than surviving another day and hoping and praying I'll one day see my family again."

Kurt placed his arm around her shoulder for a gentle and compassionate—though highly guarded—embrace. His rapidly dwindling discretion somehow barely held a wagonload of craving at bay. "You mustn't worry yourself so. You simply must hope for the very best, no matter how terribly dark and dismal things may appear—just like our situation here."

As a strong, snappy northwest wind descended upon them, and the shadows steadily lengthened, Micah summoned them to resume their exodus. They were straightaway up, marching for the coast and their designed passage to Asia Minor. Kurt took point duty and encouraged Arie to join Elena and her uncle for the balance of the day's journey, but Arie opted for the company of his longtime friend. Kurt concocted many a lame excuse to fall back to renew his flirtation, but he stopped short, fearing he might scare her off. Or, was it Marlene Knappe all over again, his freewheeling heart telling him to do one thing and his guarded German intellect another?

He wondered how Elena felt about him. Was this attention strictly a kindness, like he'd felt in the fourth grade toward dear old Miss Lutenbach?

Kurt could never want for anything more in a woman—simply matchless in every way. Stunning good looks, sweet, sensitive, compassionate, cheerful…and those eyes!

They were en route for scarcely ninety minutes when Micah announced a stay for the night, granting their exhausted bodies and troubled spirits a much-needed respite from the day's incredible demands. Micah took first watch.

Kurt fabricated a bed and headrest from branches and long grass and laid out his bedroll and blanket. His dead-tired mind would not rest until it had played back the appalling events of the past twenty-four hours. All in one day, he had shed the blood of some of the region's three belligerents: Russian, partisan, and German. He descended awkwardly to the earth, utterly spent.

He was now a renegade, on the lam like a common criminal, pursued by his own citizenry for an offense he had no way of avoiding if he were to maintain his priceless integrity. He had been taught from youth that a good reputation was desirable, but integrity was absolutely imperative. He considered that there was precious little in this world he was willing to die for, but his stand on behalf of the innocent Jewish hideaways—though positively devastating to himself and his dearest friend—was just such a one.

After a brief word on behalf of the wounded Dieter Braun and their own critical state, Kurt prayed at length for the relationship he aspired to with Elena. He reflected that not once on the journey had she demonstrated any particular social attachment, and it was his heartfelt ambition to provide her with one. As exhaustion overpowered his body, he dared to visualize her lying at his side whispering words of comfort and passion.

The sound of footsteps brought him to full alert. Incredibly, it was Elena—the very object of his entreaty of a moment ago—sliding through the moonlight.

She knelt at his side. In a hushed, sensuous voice, she asked, "Kurt, are you sleeping?"

"No, just resting," he replied, propping himself up on an elbow.

Looking caringly into his starstruck eyes, she whispered, "I wanted to tell you that I truly do admire you for the way you handled that impossible situation in the village today. I earlier expressed my gratitude, but I feel the need to add my wholehearted admiration. You are a true hero, and I'm sure God will richly bless you for your kindness."

"Thank you, Elena. It means a lot to hear you say that. You can't imagine how much I appreciated our time together today, and how I'm hoping for more of the same tomorrow, if you would favor me."

"It'll be my pleasure," she replied, extending to enclose his face with her warm hands and tenderly kissing his flushed cheek before rising and wishing him a pleasant sleep.

A hot wave of passion swept over Kurt, melting his untried heart like a block of butter exposed to the midday sun. He lay back, hands behind his head and one leg resting atop the bended knee of the other, gazing dreamily into the stars. Love-struck like never before, he gently caressed the cheek she so tenderly graced a moment ago. For sure, it would now take some time to fall off to sleep, but it was a blessed interruption.

CHAPTER TEN

Their early morning slumber was abruptly curtailed by the din of massive gunfire to the east, the dazzling flash of guns against the peaked sky a sight to behold.

Micah and Elena joined Kurt as he stretched from a satisfying sleep. Micah spoke, and she interpreted. "Your people will be under the gun today?"

"No doubt," Kurt answered. "After so long a period of inactivity, yesterday's assault was no mere probe. I'd guess we're witnessing the dawn of a grand new offensive. And I'm exceedingly grateful we're not a part of it." As Elena interpreted, Kurt swung his backpack around his shoulders. A sudden surge of sympathy came over him for his hopeless colleagues whose lives and limbs would be liberally sacrificed this day.

Micah soon had them pressing on to the coast in their bid to dodge the lamentable fate Rykert had designed. The early morning sun soon became a burden of its own. Sensing the flourishing sentiment between Kurt and Elena, Micah and Arie shared point duty.

A radiant gleam cemented to his face, Kurt gladly allowed Elena to take the conversation wherever her inventive imagination led. Their talk grew more serious as they pondered deeper philosophical matters.

"What's in store for Germany, Kurt?" she asked.

He let his head drop a little before saying, "I dare not imagine it. Possibly forever more an occupied land, carved up and administered by the communists and the Western Allies, never again free to rule herself. We've started two devastating wars this century, so I can't see them extending an olive branch when this thing has run its course."

"As long as it's free from the Nazis, that's all I care about," she responded.

"Absolutely. But I certainly hope we can delay the Russians long enough to allow the Brits and Americans to roll right over us in the West. That way we have some chance of a decent postwar life."

"There's talk of a homeland for my mother's people," Elena said, looking off in the distance. "In Palestine."

"I would be very happy for them if that's the case. I suppose that like anything else it won't come cheap. I'm sure there'll be a struggle."

"We're used to struggling. The Jews won't be denied a homeland for long—not after what we've gone through in Europe these past years. Being of mixed blood, I just don't know where I'll fit in: German Catholic or Palestinian Jew?"

"You'll succeed either way, young lady. You have character and intelligence. You can't miss."

"Thank you," she said with a smile. "A person needs reassurance every so often."

Tramping on through the elegant countryside, they gloried in the magnificence of God's creation. Lazy, towering cloud configurations added to the excellence of vibrant colors in the picturesque panorama. Why man had gone so out of his way to defile this exquisite landscape with bullets and bombs was a complete enigma.

Micah called for a mid-morning rest. Kurt and Arie displayed good cheer in a carefree conversation, not unlike that of yesterday's jubilant procession from the front lines. They were forever free from the racking horrors of the front. The previous afternoon's doom and gloom had given way to thankfulness—for being loosed from the mentally and physically taxing chains of military service.

Arie lay back on the soft grass and remarked, "I wouldn't go back to Division now if they offered me a full pardon and a promotion."

There was no talk of their ultimate destination once they'd traversed the Black Sea. They had enough to deal with in just getting that far, but there was no escaping the airy, carefree sense of freedom in the splendid summery setting.

Micah issued a caution, and Elena interpreted. "We're closing in on a village to the east that has proven a favorite partisan holdout. We must restrict unnecessary communication from here on to avoid being found out."

After a brief rest, Kurt took point and led the renegades across an open meadow to gain the refuge of forested country to the south. They struggled through dense brush and steep hills, forged a sluggish stream, and broke into a dash to cross a vast pasture covered with waist-high steppe grass before stopping to rest an hour into the afternoon. Rations were devoured and canteens drained.

As Kurt winced while eating from a tasteless tin of sardines, he was reminded that the serviceman harbors no illusions as to the contents of his ration kit. He had long since relinquished his longing for flavor, just as he concerned himself little with a bed of comfort. His sole consideration was to avert the gnawing hunger pangs which defrauded him of any peace and contentment.

Kurt found time for trivial conversation with Elena, though Micah had encouraged a few minutes rest.

Elena tore at some grass and playfully tossed it at Kurt, saying, "So tell me about your upbringing and how you landed up in Hitler's army."

Kurt plucked a blade of grass and brought it to his lips. "I was born near Bremen shortly after the Great War and raised on a modest farm. I have two older sisters and a terrific mom and dad. I guess you could say I enjoyed a wonderful upbringing, though the depression years were very hard on us. My grandfather, who passed away a couple of years ago, was a much-respected Lutheran minister, and I aspired to one day follow in his footsteps. My parents were delighted. They viewed the ministry as a preeminent calling."

"Religion plays a very big part in your life," she commented.

"Yes, my family's faith in God is much more than a passing interest—more of a fervent, lifelong commitment that affects virtually every facet of our lives."

"So this awful war put a major crimp in your plans?"

"To be sure. It was during my senior year that my life took a turn for the worse. Hitler invaded Poland and set all of Europe at war. I didn't fully share the tremendous enthusiasm of my classmates, but all the same I swelled with pride over our glorious triumphs in Poland and Western Europe. I was well aware that the Bible prohibits taking the life of another human being, but hadn't God's own people been called to take the sword to their enemies? Some months later I received my draft notice for the army and accepted my lot. After several months of back-breaking basic training, I was sent to Poland, and the rest is history."

It was then that Kurt reached for his wallet to break out the precious family photos, judging that their friendship had advanced to that point. "This is my family," he said, "my parents and my two older sisters."

"Your mom and dad are so young," she remarked, "and your sisters are simply beautiful. Are they still on the farm with your parents?"

"No. They're married with families of their own. Heidi's husband is in the navy, on a frigate somewhere in the North Sea the last I heard. Elizabeth married a doctor and lives in Potsdam. They're really great girls. You'd love them."

She asked, "You stay in close touch with your family?"

"We write often."

"Your parents worry a lot for you?"

"More than you can imagine. Dad doesn't say much in the letters, but mom says he's taking it hard. We were very close."

"And you will be again."

"You can count on it." Kurt swung his arm around her. "I can't imagine the hurt you must feel over not being able to correspond with your loved ones."

Elena lowered her head. "It seems like I'm living inside one big nightmare. But people wake up from nightmares and everything's fine again. That's the hope I have."

"I'm praying for a happy ending to your story."

Elena brought back the smile. "You're an oddity you know."

"How so?"

"You talk about spiritual matters with a passion. You put your life on the line to save others. You have principles and character not seen in other young men your age."

"Stop. You're making me blush."

She leaned forward and softly kissed his cheek, then lay back to close her eyes for a brief rest.

Kurt followed her lead, lying on the soft, warm grass, doubling his hands beneath his head, gazing thoughtfully through thick branches at the lazy, white clouds gracing the sky.

CHAPTER ELEVEN

After a refreshing hour-long rest, Micah summoned them to resume the journey.

Arie and Micah respectfully allowed Kurt and Elena more time alone by assuming point duty together again. They all understood that Rykert would not tarry in his crusade to see Kurt and Arie pay for their magnanimous stand on behalf of the hated Jews. Kurt reflected anew on the extraordinary expenditure of men and materiel on this ruthless Jewish sideshow, when the German army was so taxed in its life-and-death struggle with the Bolsheviks. Could this lunacy not have at least waited until after the subjection of the Russian army?

Sliding her arm around Kurt's, Elena was again charged with chatter. She asked, "So what was it like growing up on a farm?"

"Wonderful. But then again, farming was all I ever knew. The summers were the best: fishing, camping, no school, hot days, and warm nights. How about growing up in Hamburg? Much more exciting, I'd imagine."

"We were never bored, I'll tell you that. Daddy took us to the museums and operas and plays in the downtown parks. I guess it was a different kind of fun. You had your nature, and we had all the joyful pastimes a big city could provide. I envy your upbringing. I always dreamed of living out in the country, away from the hustle and bustle of city life."

"We aren't far from Bremen, so we got as much of the city as we wanted."

"And you probably couldn't wait to get back to the farm."

Kurt smiled his reply. Memory was like an apparition, and he wondered how, with Elena, he could so blithely contemplate his joyous past, uninhibited by the dispiriting and onerous ravages of war.

She asked, "So what's behind that devilish smile of yours?"

"Oh, nothing, really."

"Tell me."

Blushing just a little, Kurt scratched his whiskered face and said, "If you must know, I was just thinking about your age."

"Well, what did you come up with?"

"For starters, you're very mature for your age, whatever it is."

"You've covered yourself quite nicely. Go on."

"You won't hold it against me if I'm way out on this?"

She smiled. "Coward."

"Nineteen."

"Good guess. Now, was that so hard?"

"I'm sorry. I know it's not polite to ask a lady her age."

"You didn't really ask. And you? Twenty-two?"

He nodded. "Next February."

During intervals of her near-constant chatter, Kurt envisioned marriage to this beautiful young woman. He could see her assuming the day-to-day operation of his father's modest spread. He pictured the home quarter with a cozy little cottage sheltered by rolling hills to the north and a pair of immense maples out front. Smoke would drift skyward from a brick chimney while happy, healthy children cavorted about the well-kept grounds. He saw the outbuildings with contented livestock and, off in the distance, a fat field of barley ready for harvest. And there was Elena on the front porch, waving them in for dinner, her natural beauty radiating from ear to ear.

They kept conversation to a minimum, ever aware of the dangerous partisans, who they knew might even now be stalking them in hopes of inflicting a punishment far more cruel than that meted out to the recently departed SS. Kurt and Arie had witnessed firsthand evidence of macabre mutilations and torture committed by these hate-mongering guerrillas, and they'd far sooner fall victim to the callous SS. In one village they happened upon a German motorcycle courier who'd been drawn and quartered by guerrilla forces.

Shunning open ground and high spots, they traded distance for cover in an attempt to evade both the partisans and Rykert. They went unseen past an array of farmhouses of stone and mud until they eventually broke into some open terrain and followed a winding road south.

Menacing clouds dogged them all afternoon until a summer storm struck with a vengeance. The advent of heavy rains recast the ground and their footwear into a muddy mix, making their already unpleasant journey even less tolerable. Combined with the afflictions of fatigue and famishment, their lot was unenviable. The resounding thunder, fraught with dazzling flashes of white lightning, united with the heavenly downpour to make communication virtually infeasible. The hard-driving rain struck Kurt and Arie's helmets with the frequency and aggravation of a million miniature hammer blows.

It was late in the evening, with darkness laying hold on the land, that they determined to lay over for the night. Soaking wet, exhausted, and with their stomachs in open rebellion, they sprinted to an abandoned sawmill, thankful at last to escape the river of mud and scourging elements.

Upon entering the unsteady structure, Arie stopped and readied his rifle. "We're not alone here, boys. I'd recognize that grunt anywhere—wild boar." Licking his lips in joyful anticipation, he barked, "Kurt, mind the entrance. We can't let him out of here!"

Fearful of the guerrillas, Kurt added, "And no shooting!"

An incredibly entertaining game of hide-and-seek ensued, as the dagger-wielding, ravenous pair stalked the terrified beast. Much of the cloudburst had seeped in through the innumerable holes in the roof and walls, leaving the playing field muddied and exceedingly slippery. Kurt was able to dissuade the swine from escaping the building, utilizing bodily intimidation and nerve-rattling snarls, while his zealous associate, covered head to toe in mud, sweat, and chilling precipitation, led the comical pursuit. Kurt leapt and adeptly thrust his blade into the overmatched quarry, and they were soon enjoying a delicious feast.

Later in the evening, with not a hint of the moon to guide their way, Elena joined Kurt in assuming first watch. They barely held exhaustion at bay.

Kurt knew his feelings for this gorgeous young lady had all the momentum of a scouring avalanche, having now gone well past mere infatuation. She had taken his heart by storm and held him under her spell from the moment he set eyes on her! He knew he must resolve the issue, but was this the time and place?

As the rain let up, enabling them to cast off their hoods, he gently held her hands and amassed the courage to do what he knew he must—to ask the question that had been on his mind the entire day. He swallowed hard and drew a deep breath, realizing that under more sensible, peacetime conditions, he'd never so brashly forge ahead on such short notice.

He feared she would decline, sending his soaring heart crashing back to earth. His voice flittering with fear of failure, he peered ravenously into those beautiful, brown eyes. "Elena, I care a lot for you. I know that sounds strange since we've only just met. But I want to be with you—always. God willing, we'll be crossing the Black Sea in the next couple of days, but I can't bear the thought of going without you. I guess what I'm asking is—"

She leaned forward, caressed his cheeks with her downy palms, and brought her lips to his in a prolonged, captivating kiss that was followed by an affectionate embrace.

The exhilarating picture painted a thousand words, and Kurt knew he need not concern himself over her willingness to follow him, wherever he should lead. Though they had come from different worlds and had issues to resolve, each was committed to make this work. Their rapidly beating hearts left them no doubt that all obstacles would be overcome.

Micah relieved them an hour later, and the pair were soon asleep in the mill atop a carefully constructed bed of crates replete with a generous bedding of straw, furnished by the gentlemanly Aric. Even with the rain resurgent and now lashing the mill without lapse, Kurt was able to calm his soaring heart and plunge effortlessly into a bottomless sleep, virtually oblivious to the ravishing young lady at his side.

CHAPTER TWELVE

It rained hard during the night, but dawn burst with exceptional brilliance. A warm wind blew out of the west. With Arie on watch, Kurt and Elena awoke before Micah to wolf down some leftovers of last night's feast.

Kurt then lay back to deliberate on their desperate situation, fingers interlaced behind his head. Reaching to brush away a few errant strands of Elena's hair that had settled upon her lovely face, he reflected on his incredible fortune to have come to know this beautiful young lady so intimately in the midst of such dire circumstances.

He asked, "So was I dreaming last night?"

"I don't know. Tell me about it."

"It's all a little hazy, but I recall asking this dazzling young maiden if she would consider accompanying me on a semi-romantic voyage across the Black Sea, and she seemed delighted."

Elena smiled and embraced him but suddenly pushed away and jumped playfully to her feet. "Let's hit the road."

Kurt replied, "You really are a romantic, aren't you?"

She cracked a wide smile and said, "Hey, the romance is over. We took care of that last night. Time to get on with life. So, how many kids do you want?"

Kurt chuckled. "Let's slow things down just a little. I don't mean to pee on your wedding cake, but in case you haven't noticed, we have a bit of a dilemma on our hands. Remember? German army, Russian army, partisans."

Her eyes widened. "You're forgetting somebody—the Turks. I can't see them rolling out the red carpet."

A deep smile engulfed his weathered features. "Smart aleck," he replied, taking to his feet with a mighty stretch. He strolled out into the promise of a superb day of abounding sunshine. There was but a trace of wind. The clouds were high and exuded a distinct benevolence, an act of penitence following last evening's wrathful outburst. His gaze alighted on the hilltop above. "Elena, come with me. I'm going to reconnoiter the region from up on that hill."

She issued a mock salute and bounded toward him, clicking her heels on arrival.

Leaving Micah and Arie behind, they began their climb, reaching the crest by means of an animal footpath. Elena's lovely flyaway hair caught in the delicate breeze. The air was fresh from the replenishing rain, the trees and grass a glistening green. A handsome valley was unveiled before them, and on the horizon Kurt spied the Black Sea—their ticket to freedom.

Looking adoringly upon her splendid features, his face flushed with happiness and his blood aflame, he pressed her lovely lips to his. She remained in his arms as they gazed wistfully out to sea.

The rustle of leaves summoned Kurt to the ready position. He was greatly relieved to see his buddy, Arie, shuffling up the trail. "I could've shot you dead, you crazy fool!" Kurt asserted.

His hands on his hips with his back to the sun, Arie shot back, "I've observed you with a rifle, my friend, and this young lady is more at risk catching a bullet from you than I am." A wide alligator smile spread across his face as he reached for a cigarette and lit it. "You thought you could have this beautiful scenery to yourself, did you?"

Kurt waved him over for a glimpse of the Black Sea. "Come look. We're nearly there."

Arie pushed his wire-rim glasses back up the bridge of his nose and creased his dust-painted brow. "And just where is there?" he said, in a sober, toneless air. "Are we to finish out the war rustling sheep in the Turkish barrens?"

"You know I can't answer that. I'm putting one foot in front of the other, the same as you. I have no idea what the future holds, but I do know one thing. If Rykert catches up to us, we're all going to be dangling from our necks, so we need to keep moving. I know that I want to survive, and if that means running with the finish line nowhere in sight, then so be it. I wish I could change that, Arie."

"It's not your fault," Arie assured him with a pat on the shoulder. "I've replayed the whole blasted affair a dozen times, and I can't see how any of us could have handled it any differently."

Their chat was suddenly suspended by Micah's cry of distress, followed by rifle fire from the mill below. Arie and Kurt were halfway down the lush hillside in a flash, unable to view the performance but bent on securing a lead role.

More than twenty partisan horsemen swarmed the mill. Surely the fugitives had been spotted somewhere on the journey, and now this lethal band was upon them.

Kurt caught a stump and made like a boulder in a landslide for several meters, finishing up as far down the bank as Arie, but in substantially less comfort. Arie brought them to a halt in a scant clearing above the mill. They commenced spraying lead upon the partisans. Several of the mounted killers plunged awkwardly from their saddles, but others repaid concentrated fire. Arie drew Kurt's attention to Micah's bloody remains, to one side of the mill. In bad company with a blizzard of bullets smashing the vegetation around them, they took to their heels like young bucks in hunting season, surging toward the hilltop to gather a thoroughly distraught Elena, her eyes fixed with shock. "He's dead, Elena. I'm sorry," was all Kurt said as he whisked her down the wooded rear side of the knoll. Though laden with grief over the loss of Micah, Kurt was grateful for having once again cheated death.

They reached the base, sprinted parallel to the border of trees, and were at once on a collision course with three mounted partisans. Arie and Kurt put their training and years of tactical experience to good purpose, dodging enemy rifle fire and dropping to one knee to better their aim. Kurt cleared his clip after only three rounds, but Arie got off numerous shots. Two of the partisans fell from their mounts, while the other turned tail and was erased by Arie's unerring fire.

The trio secured two of the horses to expedite their escape, Elena joining Kurt on one while Arie led the way on the other. To his dismay, Kurt glimpsed a string of partisans in feverish pursuit.

As the chase progressed and the gap closed, Kurt realized they were no match for their pursuers' superior riding skills. Before he could despair, they were dealt an unexpected favor. To the west, machine guns and small arms fire rent the still air; the runaways rejoiced to see many of the partisans and their horses plummeting to the ground. Drawn by the gunfire at the mill, a modest but murderous array of armored vehicles tore across the pregnant grain field, ably dispersing the horsemen. Kurt recognized the lead armored car as that which they'd ridden in only a few days before. It was Rykert. A cigar clenched rigidly between his teeth, the SS officer blazed away with the machine gun atop the motorcar, presumably bent first on eliminating their pursuers before turning his attention on the three renegades.

CHAPTER THIRTEEN

The bloodied band of partisans was soon the least of the trio's worries, as any who remained on horseback were in complete withdrawal. Their dreaded menace, heartless SS Captain Rykert, had their undivided attention. Arie directed them to a steep incline leading back into the spacious, forest-like terrain. Machine gun fire chewed up the ground and foliage about them. Their saving grace was the rugged terrain over which the armored cars had to navigate, which greatly affected the gunners' aim.

Their horses were pressed to the limit to carry them up the grade and on toward the thicket. Machine gun fire from the lead sidecar-mounted motorcycle struck Arie's mount, thrusting him headlong to the earth.

Kurt pulled up to offer assistance.

Diving behind the shield rendered by his dying horse, Arie waved them on. "Go. I'll catch up with you," he shouted.

Arie took his revenge, striking first the passenger and then the driver, precipitating a loss of control and sending the cycle careening clumsily down a shallow ravine. Two more cycles spun out of control as Arie spent his clip.

Elena and Kurt dismounted and evaporated into the forest with Arie in ardent pursuit, thankful to have outlived the two-phased assault. The SS were certain to come after them, so they dared not rest; they bulldozed on through near-impenetrable woodland.

Some distance in, when they spotted an armored car speeding past the wood's edge, they realized Rykert was not to be outdone. As they deviated to the left to put distance between them and the SS, Kurt distinguished the drone of another vehicle evidently sent to attack their eastern flank. The woods were exceptionally narrow, and Rykert was taking full advantage to close off their escape route. They saw their lone prospect for survival—and not much of one at that—lay in squeezing through Rykert's bottleneck. Stopping to catch their breath, their faces and arms stinging from the spiny branches and bushes, they recognized the racket of foot soldiers vying to reach them from behind, which added to their perception of outright ruin.

The pitiful scene reminded Kurt of the annual Muller deer hunt, when his grandpa and father would enlist a gang of younger boys to march through a cluster of trees to spook deer and drive them toward their waiting guns.

Arie directed them farther to the south, but Kurt grabbed his arm, shouting, "We're playing right into Rykert's hands. He'll have a half-dozen men waiting for us up ahead, and we'll be mincemeat when they're done with us. We can't go on!"

Arie snapped, "So we wait here with our thumbs up our asses for them to sweep through and collect us for a firing squad back at Division?"

Kurt sucked back a deep breath, his mildly asthmatic lungs threatening mutiny. "No. We wait here under cover for the men coming up from behind and hope they pass by. Then we slip back out the way we came."

Arie and Elena were sold on his argument and straightaway secured a hiding spot.

The SS were soon all around them…and then past. Phase one of Kurt's shrewd scheme was an undisputed success.

The three started backtracking as soon as they were confident the SS had exceeded earshot, laboring back through the profuse growth nearly as swiftly as they had entered it. Kurt's spirit surged at having once again escaped the noose.

But just as the woods began to give way to the open meadow, they were brought back to earth by the awareness that their adversary had one more card to play—and it appeared to be a trump. Hearing the muffled chatter of German soldiers not more than fifty meters ahead, they plunged for cover. Rykert had situated men at the point of entry into the woodland, and it was only their undisciplined wisecracking that kept the runaways from blundering into a deadly ambush.

"Kurt, there're only a couple of them, but we've got to find a way around them quick, before Rykert becomes wise to our plan," Arie whispered. "It's now or never!"

"And no gunfire. We might as well surrender as use our firearms," Kurt added, dislodging the clip from his automatic. "If he hears shots, Rykert will be all over us like stink on manure."

"We'll make for the clearing directly to your left," Arie asserted, slinging his weapon over his shoulder. "And, Kurt, this is no time to be weighing the ethical considerations of what we have to do here," he added, withdrawing his bayonet from its sheath to press home his point that they might be required to spill more German blood to attain their freedom.

The mention of killing more of his countrymen sent a cold shiver down Kurt's spine. Shooting the SS sergeant in the village had been in self-defense. Could he do it again to save himself and his dearest friends?

The trio crawled through the undergrowth, eager to bypass this human road-block to their sought-after salvation. It was clear from their conversation that there were at least three men up ahead, and Kurt summoned the necessary fortitude to usher them all into SS hell. Yes, they were his countrymen, but if a them-or-us scenario ensued, he'd be forced to lay waste to these murdering rogues.

The panicky flight of a grouse stirred by the renegades led to one of the sentries setting off to investigate the flurry. His comrades argued that it was nothing to be alarmed over, but he carried on, much to Kurt's trepidation.

With automatic pistol primed, the SS trooper approached, consigning the threesome to deeper concealment.

Arie slowly maneuvered into a squatting posture against a tree. Exploiting it for cover, he inched his way up to prepare for the meddlesome one. If only this SS trooper had renounced his gallant endeavor and retired to the safety of his uninspired associates; instead, he was a man on a mission—his last mission. Gliding past Arie's tree, he found himself in the classic death-hold practiced in basic training: Arie's left arm pressed firmly around the man's throat while the right hand applied the blade to his exposed back.

There was little struggle, and Kurt, Elena, and Arie made for the clearing now just twenty meters ahead.

Suddenly, a voice called out. "Konrad?" With no reply, the other two SS were a house afire, bounding into the brush with rifles at the ready.

Arie gained the clearing and rolled free, but Elena and Kurt were obliged to renounce their intended breakout a mere five paces short. As the two lone shapes warily approached, Kurt reinserted his clip.

Taking dead aim at the lead man, Kurt was shocked to see Arie crashing through the trees in back of the SS and projecting himself skyward to send them sprawling. Remarkably, neither managed a shot. As they reached for their weapons, Arie was back up and at them, dispatching one with a thundering boot to the face and diving atop the other.

Kurt leapt to aid his companion and found himself standing face to face with a one-eyed SS lieutenant. At once he recognized this man as the officer from the front lines who had detained Becker. The man's mouth was a bloodied, throbbing hoard of jagged teeth, but his capacity to provide resistance appeared intact. Kurt wondered, as he lunged, why he had not employed his knife at the outset, but it was too late for conjecture as they crashed violently to the earth, rolling and tossing like mad dogs in a pit. The officer jabbed his thumbs into Kurt's eyes, but Kurt warded off the effort and reached intuitively for the blade sheathed about his right ankle. In an instant, his adversary was gyrating in agony as Kurt thrust the weapon into his right side, ending the engagement.

Kurt glanced over to behold Arie wielding a sizable stone and standing triumphantly atop his disabled and largely unconscious opponent. Arie flashed the throat-slash signal, but as Kurt looked upon the SS at his feet, shrieking and flopping about like a beached whale, he was incapable of marshalling the nerve to terminate him.

Realizing that the shouting would bring Rykert and his bloodhounds upon them, the renegades gathered their weapons, swiped a sausage and two water canteens from the SS post, and broke for the grassland, racing toward the neighboring forest some two kilometers due west. They knew Rykert was now on to their subterfuge and would be speeding back in hopes of containing them within the relatively sparse woodland they had just vacated.

Wringing wet and reeking from the onerous heat and humidity, his legs cramping in protest, Kurt recollected the last time he sprinted with such intensity. It had been in the eighth-grade track meet, where he was awarded a second place medallion. His prize this time was substantially more valuable—his life and those of his dearest friends—making this particular competition one he could ill afford to lose. Fortunately, their course was primarily downhill, and they traversed the stretch inside of five minutes. Erupting into the thicket, they paused to collect their breath and expend the precious canteens.

Rykert caught a glimpse of the renegades disappearing into the vast forest. He cupped his hands to his mouth and bellowed, "It's not over, Muller. We will find you, no matter how long it takes. You are dead men."

Kurt peered through the trees to behold the distant visage of his great antagonist. "Son of Satan," he murmured.

Elena raised her hand to still the men's heavy breathing and pointed into the thick grove. "Water. The Kogilnik River. Micah said this is the shortest route to the coast."

Without pause, and slighting the necessity to rest and refurbish their spent energies, they scrambled on, eager to let its vibrant waters escort them to the Black Sea. Footsore and weak with worry and fatigue, Kurt was the first to reach the quick but shallow waters. Tossing aside backpack and weapon, he dove in, the energy charging back into his worn and weary physique. The others followed suit.

As Kurt dragged himself from the river, he wondered if Rykert was on to their plans. Were they heading straight for the sea, or were they intent on taking the land route through Rumania? Regardless, he knew they must put time and distance between themselves and this psychopath.

Following several hours of forced marching, the sun having fully surrendered to the western horizon, Kurt raised his right arm. "We'll stop here for the night," he said, dropping his pack and weapon and snuggling the soft soil. With merely the pilfered sausage to assuage their bedeviled cravings, they were once again compelled to deal with the pangs of hunger.

Clouds densely packed and heavy with moisture drove away the last of the stars along with the thin sliver of moonlight. The dark and melancholy atmosphere was conducive to their collective state of mind. The ground, like the air, was soft and wet. A lost expression firmly implanted upon their faces, Arie and Elena slumped to the earth as if having been handed death sentences. Elena sobbed with her head buried in her hands over the loss of Micah. Once she was spent physically and emotionally, she cuddled contentedly in the crook of Kurt's arm.

Kurt kissed her forehead and tenderly stroked her silky-soft cheeks, attempting to allay her misery. "I'm sorry, Elena. Things haven't gone much according to plan."

She sat up and replied, "With my loved ones as good as dead back in Germany, Uncle Micah was all I had left. They've wiped out my entire family."

"You don't know what's happened to your family. You're imagining the worst. Now we must get some sleep. We've got a difficult day ahead of us." He laid her down and tenderly kissed her tearstained cheek.

With gloom and grief hovering above them beneath the dark and sinister clouds, they welcomed the desensitizing sleep as a deliverance from grinding misery.

CHAPTER FOURTEEN

The night was not half-done when Kurt awoke from a bad dream sopping with sweat.

Arie sat up, weapon in hand, gawking wildly into the darkness. "What is it?"

"Just a dream. I'm sorry. A nightmare really. Rykert's managed to make his way into my very sleep." He paused to run a hand through his hair. "Listen, we should make some time under cover of darkness. We must keep moving."

Arie shook his head and dislodged his glasses to massage his tired eyes. "Without Micah, we have no Russian currency, and we're virtually blind, but I take it we're still following his plan to take a boat across the sea."

Kurt nodded. "Now with the crew at gunpoint."

Elena sat up, tidied herself, and stared at the meandering river before them, her dark-shadowed eyes etched with sorrow and haunted by inner pain, her pallid unsmiling face reflecting an understandably wounded spirit. She delicately whisked back a few strands of hair with her left hand and then joined it with the other beneath her raised knees.

As Kurt helped her to her feet, she pressed her beautiful face into his chest.

"I'd give anything to bring Micah back, Elena," he said. "But he's gone. I'm truly sorry, but we have to go on now without him."

She granted a forced smile while readying herself to follow his lead, hunger vying for her attention.

A handful of stars reappeared. The air was warm and wet. There was virtually no communication as they trudged off into the night through a labyrinth of nearly impassable bush. Small, biting bugs added to their discomfort.

After calling for a pause to refill their canteens, Kurt said, "Rykert will undoubtedly be looking to intercept us somewhere along the way. But where? What do you think, Arie?"

"I'm more concerned about losing the cover of the forest. You see that big open field dead ahead?"

Elena pointed skyward to note the first feeble rays of a reddish orange dawn. "And it'll soon be full light."

Kurt's voice grew soft. "We have no food, and the longer Rykert has to secure assistance from the local military and civilian population, the worse it'll be for us. There looks to be a small town, doubtless Tatarbunary, at the conjunction of the river and that winding road dead ahead. From there, we should be able to commandeer a boat to Turkey. Unless one of you has a better plan."

Stepping out from the cover of trees, Arie craned his neck and pointed to a lengthy procession of men and machines. "Look, up ahead on the road. German army. A full battalion."

Kurt strained his eyes and added, "Maybe an entire division, heading straight for town. A redeployment?"

"I'd guess a full scale retreat," replied Arie. "Just our luck. We're sailing straight into half the bloody German army."

"This could be a blessing in disguise, Arie. You and I will be nearly impossible to distinguish from the horde once we reach the town, and we'll only need concern ourselves with Elena's passage. Let's tell them that you and I are under orders to deliver our partisan prisoner here into town."

"Sounds good to me," Arie replied, leading them toward the town.

Kurt asked, "Do you know anything about boats, Arie? We may need to just out-and-out steal one if the crew isn't around or is reluctant to take us on."

"Are you kidding? I've never been in anything larger than a rowboat. How about you?"

"Nothing at all. I guess we'll just have to make like British buccaneers and force their hospitality."

"Wait. I may be able to help," Elena responded, downcast but forcing a grin. She produced a gold watch from her shirt pocket and handed it to Kurt. "This will be more than enough to pay our passage."

Kurt leaned forward to kiss her in recognition of her extraordinary sacrifice. He then released the back of the watch to examine a family photo and looked up to observe tears welling up in her eyes and trickling down her unblemished cheeks. He realized that the watch was her final bond with her precious family, and he drew his arms around her for a sympathetic embrace. "It's all right, Elena, we'll find another way. I won't allow you to part with this," he said, as he pressed it into her hands.

"No. No, it's the only way. Otherwise, we are thieves and criminals no better than the SS, and I will not disgrace myself. Accept it now or I will have no part in your escape."

Reluctantly, Kurt pocketed the cherished timepiece, realizing how much this lamentable conflict had cost innocent individuals such as this gracious young lady. Whoever declared that the power of love was greater than hate had not encountered all of life in those despondent days on the Eastern Front. Here, it was the law of the jungle, where only the strongest—or perhaps the very lucky— survive against the widespread enmity. And strong they would be. He was now more resolved than ever to see this beautiful young lady to safety.

With the sun fashioning a glorious reappearance, they made their way to Tatarbunary, bruised and battered, torn and tattered, hunger snapping at their heels.

CHAPTER FIFTEEN

Tatarbunary appeared to be what Kurt's father would refer to as a choice spot for an enema—should the Almighty so decide this old world was in need of one. Bleak and grubby, its potholed and muddied streets were flanked by drawn and dilapidated buildings like those of a concentration camp.

Their pace was swift but not frantic as they made for the pier, where one lone craft bounced on the waves. They concluded that the uninterrupted column of slovenly soldiers, intermingled with a handful of fleeing civilians pulling over-laden carts, was part of at least an entire division in headlong retreat.

Scarcely halfway across the open ground, the fugitives witnessed a panic among the retreating troops. They looked skyward to see three Soviet fighters commence a strafing attack. Arie and Elena dove for cover, but perceiving the opportunity they were looking for, Kurt made a mad dash for the boat. Hot on the heels of the three MiGs came two more, serving up another helping of death and dismemberment and tearing up the ground beneath them. Sounds of suffering filled the air as the strafing exacted a terrible toll on the defenseless foot soldiers, with men tumbling and toppling in agony.

A stricken soldier collapsed before them, swirling in torment in a deepening pool of his own blood. Mercifully, he'd not last long. Not having Kurt and Arie's experience in such gruesome matters, Elena nearly fainted at the sight.

Momentarily losing sight of Arie, Kurt glanced around to see him scrambling in the direction of a forlorn little girl, who stood next to a crumpled figure—doubtless her mother—who was floundering amidst the unsympathetic traffic. Arie swooped up the woman and rushed her to the protection of a mud and stone hut. Kurt raced back to take the toddler in his arms and follow Arie's lead, relinquishing them there in the care of other panic-ridden civilians. Arie had a mind to offer further assistance, but common sense drove it away.

Within a few paces of the boat, their hearts heaving at the prospect of deliverance, they were brought to a halt by a sober-minded sergeant of the Military Police, brandishing a machine gun, his eyes narrowed with suspicion.

"Who are you? Where are you going?" he barked.

Kurt was certain this fellow had seen enough deserters in his day to recognize a possible fit here, what with their apparent objective the forlorn boat a stone's throw ahead. He was convinced, also, that Elena's presence was cause for concern.

"Corporal Muller and Private Schonert," Kurt responded. "Eighty-eighth Division."

"And the girl?"

"A partisan prisoner. Our commander, Captain Rademaker, told us to take her here and that he'd be along shortly."

"All right then, follow me," he dictated in a croaking voice and waving an ape-like hairy hand through the air. He turned and galloped toward a cluster of bombproof concrete buildings.

While the Soviet aircraft carried on raising hellish havoc, the three traded anxious glances in search of a solution to this latest predicament. If they turned and ran for it, they'd be giving themselves away and inviting grievous attention from this man and his cohorts, whom they saw more of now, directing the panic-stricken traffic in the midst of the enemy aerial attack. If they went along with him, they'd likely land in a tub of trouble. If they shot him, he'd be dead and they'd be free to carry on to the craft and away from all this affliction.

Yes, the third proposal was assuredly the most sensible. No one would suspect a thing, what with the widespread bedlam and gunfire. But, as the sergeant turned and braked to consider their reluctance to join him in the protected concrete structures, they were powerless to forfeit this man's life. Kurt waved the others on to follow the MP.

Enemy bombers enlisted in the free-for-all, and clamor and confusion amplified their unease as the three fugitives were led to a sizable, converted warehouse. It appeared to facilitate the nerve center of command and communications.

The large-boned, barrel-chested MP was a burly brute: weather-beaten bulldog face, meaty forearms, neck of a bull—not someone you'd choose to be at odds with. Bushy black eyebrows impounded a pair of dark, permanently brooding eyes set in cratered alligator skin. It was obvious that, with the passing of time, a portion of his chest had fallen away into his belly, but there was no mistaking the brute strength.

Kurt, Arie, and Elena were confident in entering the structure that, as was evident from the unsuspecting noncommissioned officer leading them, the MPs were not on the lookout for them. Nonetheless, they kept a watchful eye for the dreaded SS attire.

Kurt felt a jab in his ribcage as they were ushered toward a dimly lit compartment in the back, Elena seeking his attention. She doubled over in feigned discomfort and cupped her hands beneath her mouth. Kurt and Arie were at once on to her hoax.

Arie shouted, "The girl is about to lose her lunch, Sergeant."

"Get her outside now, or I'll have you two down on your knees licking it up," he snapped.

As soon as they had turned the corner Kurt grasped Elena's arm and flashed an approving grin. Bursting out the door, their hearts sank. The boat was making a run for the open sea. Snarls of agony upon their faces, they stood dumbstruck amid the human wreckage and the disappearing whine of an ill-fated Soviet fighter hit by antiaircraft fire. To their added despair, the person who was answerable for their not being on that confounded vessel, the obtruding MP, appeared at the door bearing an acidy air of suspicion.

The remaining planes regrouped and headed east, bloated from their German feast; with bowed heads the threesome submitted to their misfortune and withdrew inside to act out their deception. They would be obliged to carry on as before and wait for another boat and another opportunity—clearly the best of a bad lot of alternatives.

The building was crawling with dust and an array of hair-raising creatures, cheerless to say the least, with scant furnishings. Their concern that Rykert or one of his associates would happen along was uppermost in their minds as they walked uncertainly into the dingy compartment housing the Military Police.

On a table against one wall lay a coffee-stained map, wrinkled like a rhino. Three thumbtacks pressed into the tattered corners of a territorial map kept it from collapsing to the cement floor. Yet another wall featured a dusty, crooked picture of the *Führer*, his arm extended in a familiar pose.

The MP sat at a makeshift desk swarming with crumpled paper and defaced file folders. A near-empty bottle of Schnapps stood amid the indescribable clutter, next to an overturned shot glass and a piece of nibbled cheese.

Elena did her utmost to appear as though she had just tossed up everything but the kitchen sink, as Kurt cordially extended his right hand to the MP. "The name's Kurt Muller. I want to thank you, Sergeant, for seeing us to safety here," he said.

The brute refused Kurt's hand but motioned to a dusty bench. "Sit down and shut up," he snapped. "You could have gotten me cut to ribbons out there, making me wait for your sorry backsides," he grumbled with a withering glance while he fumbled for a cigarette from a pack half-spilling out from his shirt pocket. "I thought you were some cursed runaways making for the open sea. I had a mind to shoot you dead and ask my questions later," he added, pointedly stabbing an index finger in their direction while hurling his grubby boots up on the desk.

Kurt answered in trumped-up respect, "I beg your pardon, Sergeant, but we simply panicked and wanted to get as far off that road as possible. We've been up to our rumps in partisans for a couple of days now and could sure use some food and rest before my commander arrives to fetch us back to Division."

"You do have your orders on you, Corporal?" he inquired, his eyes narrowing as he dropped his feet and uncorked the schnapps to half-fill a dirty glass.

"No, sir. Our platoon was en route here with our prisoner when we were set upon by partisans," Kurt explained, fabricating his defense as he went along. "Captain Rademaker told Arie and me to take her on ahead, saying he would meet us here in Tatarbunary when they had beaten them off. If you don't buy our story, you can wait for him to get here, any time now."

The MP pushed himself up, strode out from behind the desk, and gestured toward Elena. The sergeant tossed back the liquor and snarled, "What's so important about this one that your captain doesn't just blow her head off and be done with it?"

"I guess she must have some valuable information that the captain wants to get at first," said Arie, nervously wringing his hands.

The hard-boiled MP turned his attention upon Kurt. "Well, just the same, I don't want any of you out of my sight until we've been able to verify your story. Understood?"

"Perfectly understood," Kurt answered.

The MP poached one more predatory glance at Elena, making no attempt at being discreet, running his hard, hungry eyes up and down her flawless frame. He drew one last drag on his cigarette, butted it out on an empty plate, and cleared his throat with the tobacco-roughened grunt of the chain smoker. "Good. Now if you'll follow me, I'll show you to the mess tent. Maybe we can even manage to scare you up a cot or two. Leave your weapons here."

Kurt and Arie propped their rifles against the bench, and the threesome came to their feet, trailing the sergeant into the courtyard behind the building. A bulky canvas shelter emitted savory smells of ham and eggs and other delicacies long forgotten. Their host paused and motioned them into the tent, but—to their alarm—seized Elena and pulled her aside.

"Enjoy your breakfast, boys. I'll be doing a little interrogating of my own," he said with a wink and distorted smile that left Kurt in a mixed state of fear and anger.

Elena was the picture of despair, sallow and sunken eyed. She struggled along as one about to be blindfolded at the wall and shot, as the portly sergeant shoved her back into the building.

For a moment, Arie and Kurt were speechless; they faltered to try to deal constructively with the crisis at hand.

"Sergeant," Kurt spouted as he reached the doorway, "I don't think our captain will take too kindly to you having your way with the prisoner. He made it clear she was not to be violated."

Turning and dislodging his cap to run a hand through his sparse crop of stringy, brown hair, the MP quizzed in a tart, whisky-soaked voice, "And just what is he saving her for, Corporal?"

"For himself, I would imagine," Kurt replied, swallowing hard, shifting his weight from one foot to the other. "He knows how stunning she is and how…that every mother's son would love to have a go at her. So he made it unmistakable that no one—and that means you, sir—is to lay a hand on her."

The sergeant cleared his throat, clenched his huge hands, and glared. "Corporal, your half-assed threats are an insult to me. To be honest with you, I'm growing very suspicious of your lame story. If my hunch is correct, that meal could well be your last. So eat hearty and mind your own business, or I'll put you both under guard right this minute. As for your Captain Rademaker, what he doesn't know won't hurt him. Understood?"

The sergeant shot them a dismissive gesture as he led away the lovely young lady Kurt had come to love with all his heart.

Elena shuffled off with a stricken look.

His mouth cavernous, Kurt stared in disbelief, searching for an answer to this latest crisis, yet unable to cope with the stress and hardship poured out upon him these last days. It was as though a full company of 88 mm cannons was firing inside his head.

CHAPTER SIXTEEN

Arie shook Kurt out of his stupor and exclaimed, "Come on. We've got to do something and do it now!"

Kurt nodded and struck off in pursuit of the love of his life and the filthy swine who was about to defile her. The MP was as good as dead, though Kurt didn't yet know the exact method or means.

Arie and Kurt accelerated to keep pace as the MP manhandled Elena to the front entrance. They reached the doorway and watched him prod her along toward a stable across the street.

As they started after them, a hawk-nosed, gangly officer stuck out a bony arm. "You two, follow me. We need more help with the wounded on this truck."

What could they do but accede to his authority, forcing them to postpone the release of dear Elena? As they climbed into the dark and canvassed transport, Kurt stood petrified, eyes wide with alarm, by a most upsetting sight. He swapped agonizing glances with his colleague, who himself had a ghostly countenance. It was neither the mangled bodies nor the stench of marred flesh that horrified them; rather, the sinister SS insignia stitched to their bloodied garb was what froze them in their tracks. The next sound they heard was the monstrous voice of the archenemy, Rykert, coming around from the front of the truck. Sternly, he warned the soldiers to extend his men the greatest of care. Fortunately, the canopied truck limited visibility, saving Kurt and Arie from detection. The men beneath them were the unfortunate victims of yesterday's deadly encounter, and Kurt flinched as he pondered the frightful repercussions of them being exposed.

"You two, get with it!" bawled the gangly one standing next to Rykert, sensing their reluctance to involve themselves in the distasteful endeavor.

Shrouded by the canvas backing and with their backs to the officers, Arie and Kurt chose one of the remaining wounded, striving to quell the billowing disquiet within. Each grasped an arm of a man afflicted with a bullet wound to his left knee. They pressed his arms around their heads and walked down an improvised ramp and straight past the one responsible for their misfortune, praying earnestly they'd not be recognized.

Kurt drew a colossal sigh of relief as they shuffled the wounded man through a maze of corpses and into a cheerless room, where surgeons and medics cared for the injured flocking their way. Kurt was reminded once more of the horrors of this tragedy as he considered men writhing in ear-piercing agony. They were directed by an adjutant to a large table in the center of the room, where they watched, in disgust, a leg amputation. The beleaguered SS man in their care perceived his fate and struggled for release. It was all Arie and Kurt could do to force him along to his appointment with the surgeon.

His ranting and raving attracted much attention. One of the disabled SS—specifically, the lieutenant Kurt had fought hand to hand with—boosted himself up from a nearby table and wildly railed on. "Traitors. Murderers. Arrest them, I tell you. Arrest them!" Fortunately, he was only half-coherent, the result of a massive dose of pain killer.

As he and Arie handed over their charge to the waiting orderlies, Kurt had the presence of mind to explain away the lieutenant's actions to a growing number of inquisitive onlookers. "At least he's getting a little better. He mistook us for a couple of barmaids when we first came upon him in the truck a few minutes ago."

At this, a weary surgeon summoned an orderly to administer another dose of the desensitizing sedative, and their would-be squealer was ushered off into a whole new world of bliss.

Kurt and Arie snuck out through a side door, down a splintered stairway, and around the corner, away from the extraordinary peril and on to save Elena. Keeping a watchful eye out for Rykert, they hastened toward the stable. Kurt deftly withdrew his bayonet, bracing for the grisly task to come. He was surprised at the composure with which he contemplated the demise of the ill-mannered pig.

Arie pulled at Kurt's arm and gestured toward the pier. "Look, the cargo vessel's come back. We must hurry."

Kurt swung open the stable entry and was flabbergasted to see the sergeant lying on the floor, groaning and gripping his aching crotch. He noticed a nasty gash atop the poor devil's balding head. His eyes were blackened with dirt.

The sunlight from the yawning doorway revealed Elena slumped against a stall, whimpering, the sergeant's revolver in one hand and a bloodied shovel in the other. Her garments were badly torn, but she had saved herself from the intended rape.

Kurt rushed to embrace her while Arie secured the door. She continued sobbing while he extended comfort and praised her for standing up to the immoral louse. He took her face in his hands. "We've got to get out of here, Elena. The boat's come back. The sergeant will soon be missed, and Rykert's here too."

The MP raised himself on wobbly knees and formed a fist to deliver a blow, but Kurt took the shovel from Elena's grasp and swung it with deadly force. The MP slammed against the stable and fell to the floor, dead as the dirt he lay on.

CHAPTER SEVENTEEN

Arie led his companions into the sunlight, all the while on the lookout for the dreaded captain. Battered buildings and blasted vehicles lay smoldering about the rubbled and cratered ground littered with an occasional corpse. A shabby old woman, delirious with heartache, knelt at the side of her deceased mate.

Kurt, Arie, and Elena made their way to the pier, scurrying from one building to another, thankful that the two-man crew was on board, reclining comfortably against sacks of grain seed. The older crewman had the semblance of a gorilla, heavy-jawed with a low forehead and protruding lips. His leather-faced sidekick featured the high Slavic cheekbones prevalent in these parts and a glassy-eyed, gap-toothed leer.

Elena explained to the crew in Ukrainian that they were in need of transport, and Kurt produced their fare in the form of the inestimable gold watch. The seamen's eyes sparkled as they appraised it, nodded their approval, and rattled off something to Elena as they scurried onto the pier.

Arie and Kurt dropped to the deck of the craft to conceal themselves. Elena explained, "They went to radio ahead to a Turkish port across the sea to obtain authorization to enter. They're not ordinarily permitted there, so otherwise we'd be arrested—or worse yet, blown out of the water by the unobliging Turks."

Kurt nodded and leaned back. "We'll soon be free of this sorrowful European holocaust, Arie. The nightmare is over. I have to admit, though, that I expect total confusion once we cross this body of water. What's to become of us is anyone's guess. But I'll take my chances in Turkey as opposed to this madness."

Decked out in a boyish grin as if he had been brought back from the dead, Arie reached to grip Kurt's hand. "We'll jump off that bridge when we get to it. We did it, man. We really did it. We'll have a few stories to tell the grandkids, eh?"

"Yeah, it appears we've gotten the better of Rykert, not to mention a troop of bloodthirsty partisans. Our lives haven't exactly been dull these past days." Kurt turned away and lowered his head. "My only regret is that Rykert survived to go on with his murdering. I should have let you shoot the fatherless swine. What was I thinking?"

"Your problem is that you've never made the adjustment here. I'm surprised all the death and suffering hasn't convinced you by now that you can't always play by the rules, my friend."

Elena stood gawking at an aging permit dangling from the wall of the steering compartment, her pretty face twisted in perplexity. "Kurt, come look at this. It's a permit authorizing this craft to dock in Russian and Turkish ports at any time. Why do you think they told me they needed to radio ahead for approval?"

Kurt's eyes focused on the permit, then on Elena, and lastly on Arie, who was up on his feet with knife in hand.

"Get this piece of crap moving! I'll cut the ropes!" Arie charged.

Elena and Kurt swung into action, realizing that Rykert must have prepared every boat commander up and down the coast for their arrival. There was no time to spare. Fortunately, the key was in the ignition, and Kurt labored to turn over the timeworn engine.

The boat came to life just as shots rang out. Kurt whirled to see Arie crouching for cover as a half-dozen SS men came charging their way. Arie slashed the restraining ropes on one side of the boat, but the others were securely in place.

Kurt grasped his dagger while Elena assumed the controls, but as he lunged to help sever the remaining lines, he heard an all-too-familiar moan.

Arie recoiled and doubled over, threatening to plunge head first into the murky waters.

Kurt stretched to intercept his fall, easing him back into the vessel, altogether oblivious to the enduring gunfire.

"No, no," Arie bawled, gaping incredulously at a pair of bullet holes in his lower chest. His teeth chattering, his eyes blood red but emptying, and his chest surging, his entire body locked into the fetal position.

Kurt's heart ached, his mind raced, and his eyes expanded with a sickening wave of terror. He supported Arie's limp frame in his arms and placed his left hand over the oozing punctures, as if to arrest the flow of blood. "Please God, don't let him die!" he wailed, his breath catching in his throat.

Elena knelt at their side, engulfed in sheer terror.

Tears formed in his eyes as Kurt embraced Arie.

The SS arrived at a position immediately overhead on the pier.

"You're...you're OK, Arie," Kurt stammered, unremitting panic in his voice. "We'll get you...we'll get you to a doctor real soon. Hang in there, old buddy."

But Arie was dead.

His eyes clouding over, Kurt lovingly passed his hand over Arie's snowy white face to close his hollow, unlit eyes. He burst into a strangled cry over the departure of his faithful friend. Yes, he had gone—and with him a good measure of Kurt's desire to go on with this difficult life.

The SS rushed aboard to confiscate their weapons, and Kurt heard a familiar voice. Feeling strangely disembodied in his agony, he turned to behold the unsightly object of his undying dread and inexhaustible contempt—Captain Rykert.

The captain regarded their misfortune with intense satisfaction, his face forming a proud, heartless sneer. Standing behind him, the treacherous swine ogled the timepiece they'd been offered in good faith. Rykert turned to allot them the promised reward for the renegades' apprehension, a handful of Russian coins, and the seamen boarded their vessel.

Kurt gulped down a measure of inner anguish as Rykert flashed a scornful grin.

In a voice cold as death, the captain gloated, "Did I not tell you, Muller, that I would track you down? It was only a matter of time."

Kurt's eyes narrowed with contempt. His face grew hot as he retaliated in an utterance strangled with emotion. Happy at last to extend this repulsive creature the disrespect he so richly deserved, he blurted, "You couldn't track a wounded elephant in the snow, you mindless moron!"

Rykert's eyebrows raised, and his head shifted to one side at Kurt's insolence. "You know, you really must do something about that infantile display of remorse; it simply doesn't befit a man of your proven stature. Your murdering friend there got just what was coming to him." A malicious smirk preceded a contemptuous laugh as Rykert's gaze shifted to Elena. "And what do we have here? No, let me guess; one of your beloved Jews from the village, I would imagine. You seem a bit of a romantic, Muller, and very much a fool. A daring and compassionate fool, but a fool nonetheless. Germany will be none the worse off without you."

Having concluded Kurt's eulogy, Rykert reached for a machine gun from a subordinate.

Kurt eyed the black-hearted knave fearfully with the helplessness of a fly entangled in a spider's web. Then, he embraced Elena as one would a small child. He closed his eyes at the burst from Rykert's MP43, but wheeled around in disbelief to see the ignominious Russian seamen riddled with bullets and tumbling awkwardly onto the bow of their ship.

"Get the reward and watch," snorted Rykert, and two SS boarded the vessel. Turning his attention back upon Kurt and Elena, he said, "Fooled you, didn't I?"

"Get it over with, you pompous ass!" Kurt snarled, his eyes seething and his teeth gritted. "I've resigned myself to dying; it's having to sit here and tolerate your idiotic banter that disturbs me!"

Rykert received the reward and watch from his men and then ordered the lot of them back to town, with a further command to one of his subordinates which Kurt could not make out. He examined the gold watch and opened it to regard the portrait of Elena's family.

Her lips quivering and choked to the point that her voice began to break, Elena declared, "They are my family…or at least, they *were* my family." She looked up at him for an instant before bowing her head to hide the coming tears. "I assume your colleagues back in Hamburg have seen to their extermination by now," she added, a touch of anger seeping into her voice.

Astonished with Elena's mastery of German, Rykert shook his head, shifted his coldhearted gaze, and wagged a finger. "You two exhibit a very low opinion of me," he alleged in a striking understatement, hardly more than a whisper. "You think me a barbarian, a creature without thought or sensitivity. Truthfully, I'm not overly drawn to my present assignment and have more than once requested transfer to a frontline unit. But my superiors consider me entirely indispensable in my current capacity."

Enraged at the sickly self-justification, his hands balled into fists, his chin thrust out, Kurt stormed, "Bullshit. Don't dare rationalize it away, Rykert! You're a heartless, sadistic criminal, and you'll pay for your atrocities one day!"

The captain's eyes grew cold as he tossed back his shoulders and shot a finger out at Kurt. "I'll have you know I am a man of honor and a soldier like you. But, unlike you, I submit to my orders, no matter how distasteful they may be. And, unlike you, I performed my duty in that village the other day!"

"Duty?" Kurt snapped, taking to his feet, leaving Arie's body to Elena's care. With his index finger raised, his blood on the boil, and unmistakable disdain in his voice, he raved, "You call butchering innocent women and children a duty? Tell me, Captain, what is duty in the absence of honor?"

"You answer my question first, Muller. What is honor in the absence of duty? And who made you my judge? I crap more honor every day than you'll ever know in a lifetime! And you—who are you to point a finger, after running off like a common thief, hiding out in the woods, afraid to face the consequences of your actions?"

"I am not afraid to face anything that is honorable and just. Grant me a fair trial in a peacetime courtroom, and I'll be there to prove my innocence. Now, get it over with, or so help me I'll come drive that piece down your throat!"

With this, Kurt knew he had breathed his last. The captain raised his weapon, and Kurt knelt to press Elena close, recalling the unparalleled rapture she had brought him these past days. He was perfectly content that this blessed realization would be his final conscious thought.

Another eruption of the machine gun left them—still alive. Unnerved, they observed with wonder the remaining restraining ropes blasted to shreds; they had been set completely free from the pier. Just what kind of depraved cat and mouse game was he playing? Rykert was squeezing every last bit of perverted pleasure from this pathetic episode.

An SS staff car pulled up at the pier and stayed just long enough for a young skin-and-bones Russian toddler with ruddy complexion and azure eyes to jump from the passenger's seat and run toward Rykert.

The captain drew him near, placed his arm around him, and whispered something in his ear. Turning to Kurt and Elena, he said, "I would like you to meet someone very special to me. This is my son, Albert. His mother was a local girl. When the partisans learned of our relationship, they did away with her...slowly and very painfully. Thankfully, Albert had been playing at a neighbor's home, where he was kept safe and cared for until I returned some time later. If the partisans catch up with him they will kill him, Muller. I'm sure you can appreciate my concern."

"And...you're willing to spare our lives in exchange for seeing him to safety," Kurt concluded.

"Precisely. I've come to terms with the fact that we will not win this war. Even if I manage to survive the fighting, I'm not likely to get off with a slap on the wrists after what I've done here. I'll either be dead or rotting in an Allied prison—or, if I'm lucky, running for my life in some forgotten part of the world. In any case, I have no life to offer my son. But you—you could take him away to safety somewhere in the West and find him a good home. Couldn't you? I'm not asking you to do it for my sake, but think of the boy and your own lives. You know I'm not going to allow you to leave here alive without him."

Without further deliberation, Kurt reached to put a hand on the pier to secure the boat from drifting out to sea and extended his hand to the ill-fated lad.

Rykert hugged his son and directed him toward Kurt.

The boy, who had known misery well beyond his years, lost control of his emotions as Kurt took him in his arms and passed him on to Elena.

As the boat slowly drifted from shore, Rykert placed the watch in the sack containing the reward money, pitched them to Elena, and then inexplicably tossed his weapon to Kurt. "The high seas are full of treachery, Muller. You may need this."

Kurt was utterly dumbfounded. Rykert, his nemesis, stood defenseless on the pier. Kurt slowly raised the machine gun and engaged the contemptible creature eye to eye. He considered ending his pathetic existence, but something restrained him.

Rykert declared with a wicked smile, "I knew you couldn't do it, Muller. You're just too much the honorable gentleman. We may meet again someday, my friend. I trust it will be under more pleasant circumstances." His dark, war-hardened eyes fell one last time upon the teary-eyed little boy before he marched back into town.

His face reflecting irreparable damage, Kurt slumped into Elena's waiting arms and gazed despairingly at his lifeless friend, then at the sobbing lad, and finally at the love of his life. Sadness and fury were at work within, vying for mastery of his emotional state.

Whatever the case, they had once more escaped the wrath of a practiced SS assassin. A moment later, Kurt was at the throttle with Elena at his side, hugging him and wailing uncontrollably as they made for the open sea. They were, at last, unfettered by the monstrous afflictions of war, but their immeasurable sorrow over the loss of Arie and Micah put to chase any thought of celebration.

CHAPTER EIGHTEEN

Rykert's money enabled Kurt and Elena to purchase supplies for a harrowing voyage across the Mediterranean to neutral Spain, where they lived out the remaining months of the war. It was there they married.

Little Albert became a permanent member of the family. Initially, they reasoned it the humane thing, but soon they were incurably in love with the little guy, and there was just no parting with him.

During long days working in the fields and vineyards of southern Spain, they had opportunity to reflect on their amazing adventure. Physically, there were no scars, but the mental anguish over the loss of Micah and Arie proved most difficult. There wasn't a day that Kurt failed to think about Arie and the warm bond they had built during their time together in Russia, and Elena shared with Kurt many happy stories about her Uncle Micah.

Added to this was the fact they were now refugees, having been driven to disavow their citizenship. And Elena was never at peace over the plight of her beloved family in Germany, who she still hoped might somehow have managed to cheat the Nazi executioners.

For the duration of their time in Spain, they were continually on guard for the persistent customs officials, who were none too eager to extend a warm welcome to a pair of ill-fated German expatriates. But that was nothing compared to the life-threatening variety of dangers they'd endured in Eastern Europe.

In January of '45, their shifting fortunes took a definite turn for the better through a chance meeting with an immigrant journalist named Hannes Brandenburg. He had left Düsseldorf in the midthirties to cover the Spanish Civil War and elected to stay on in the beautiful seaboard town of Alicante. Their acquaintance evolved into an unfailing friendship, and he played a significant role in rebuilding Kurt and Elena's well-being. He put them up in his humble home, helped frustrate the pesky immigration officers, and found jobs to meet their basic needs.

Hannes kept them abreast of the war, and they weren't at all surprised to see Germany besieged from east and west as it grievously staggered beneath the combined hammer blows of the omnipotent Allies. They reacted with mixed sentiments—happy for the Western Allies' approach, but disheartened by the Soviets' eastern onslaught. They understood that the issue had been decided in the Allies' favor years ago, and so they anxiously awaited the end, be it merciful or otherwise. Enough blood, good and bad, had been spilt. The German people's day of reckoning was on the horizon. One day in May, Hannes returned with a copy of the local paper sporting a huge headline proclaiming Germany's unconditional surrender. They mourned over the war's absolute futility; so many had been thoughtlessly offered up on the bloody altar of fallen humanity, all of them victims of unfathomable savagery.

Kurt and Elena were free at last to travel to war-ravaged Germany, and they craved the opportunity to see precious family. Their savings secured passage to southern Germany and on to Bremen, where Kurt's parents afforded him a hero's reception. A ten-day family reunion ensued, with Kurt's sisters descending upon the farm with their own families to welcome home their beloved brother. The experience was even better than Kurt had imagined it could be, much more than he had dared hope for during his time away from his precious loved ones. Elena was warmly welcomed into the family and made to feel as though she had always been a member. Little Albert instantly gained grandson status and spent many a happy day with Kurt's parents.

The following weeks saw numerous trips to nearby Hamburg to locate Elena's family, but to no avail. It was only when they mustered the nerve to visit the Bergen-Belsen concentration camp, with its idle gas chambers and grisly crematoriums, that the awful truth of their demise unfolded. Elena took it terribly hard and found it most difficult to accept life in the new Germany. However, wallowing in self-pity wasn't the answer. She grieved with that same stupendous passion with which she experienced all else, and then she resolved to get on with their new lives.

Kurt and Elena vowed that, in spite of his hideous bloodline, Albert would never feel the sting of rejection. They loved him as their own.

Kurt was anxious to uncover Rykert's whereabouts, should he have survived the war. Neither Allied intelligence nor the renowned Austrian Documentation Center could assist him, other than a best guess that he'd followed the normal Nazi route to freedom in South America, where so many of the godless Nazi riff-raff lived in luxury with stolen goods such as gold and valuable art. Kurt took heart in Isaiah's proclamation, "There is no peace for the wicked."

That the German people suffered horrendously was evident in Kurt and Elena's grueling trips to Hamburg, where they witnessed the appalling devastation inflicted by the unfeeling Allied bombers. Not a street had escaped their fury. Most inhabitants existed without a roof or bare walls to shield from the elements. Bridges, factories, hospitals, schools, and all means of transportation lay shattered. During one particularly morbid ten-day period of incessant bombing, more than forty thousand had lost their lives, mostly in the firestorms that followed the merciless pounding. Kurt likened it to gutted and ghostly Kharkov in '43, where nary a structure was left untouched by the horrific terror brought to bear by German and Russian armies bent on its capture. It seemed like yesterday that Kurt's family had looked on with fascination at prideful Nazi rallies parading down Hamburg's stately avenues, with Adolf Hitler saluting victoriously from his Mercedes.

The news coming out of what became East Germany made Kurt and Elena ever so happy to have settled in the west. The conquering Russians exacted a barbarous vengeance upon those unable to avoid their path of wholesale havoc. Stalin had made it clear that only the unborn are innocent. Murder and molestation accompanied the unmerciful pillaging of every city and town the Soviet army happened upon. The German people reaped a whirlwind of calamity. Some twenty million terror-struck civilians fled to the west in what was thought to be the world's greatest mass migration. By war's end, starvation had reduced some to eating cats and dogs. Looting was rampant. People exchanged priceless heirlooms for food. Flies, rats, and lice had a field day.

Kurt reflected that never in the annals of human history were a people called to bear such a burden of reproach as the Germans. Governed by Nazism, the silent majority had turned a blind eye and a deaf ear to all that was wrong, looking the other way while some of their countrymen plumbed the very depths of human degeneracy. Germany was left with a diabolical legacy never to be forgotten, much less forgiven; one can place only so much of the blame at the feet of the despot. All must give account for allowing the psychopath to lead them into such debauchery.

Hitler's fickle affinity seemed directly linked to his subjects' capacity to fulfill his absurd aspirations. The German *Volk* were, in his perverted judgment, merely instruments of the state to be expended at will for the greater glory of the nation.

Kurt recalled reading Hitler's own words: "What is life? Life is the nation. The individual must die anyway; beyond the life of the individual is the nation." And Kurt remembered how the maniac had cautioned long before his rise to power that, "Even if we cannot conquer, we shall drag the whole world into destruction with us." How sadly prophetic!

The truth of the Holocaust was soon common knowledge throughout the country. The Nazi treatment of the Jewish people had been abominable. Considered subhuman and likened to lice, Jewish citizens had been slowly severed from society. Beginning in 1938, all German schools had been closed to Jews, while their places of worship and business were decimated, their doctors and lawyers barred from practice. Jews were branded like cattle with demeaning tattoos and forced to wear a yellow star to mark their inferiority and subservience. Rape and brutal beatings were commonplace.

Kurt proudly shared with Elena an incident involving a trip to Bremen prior to the outbreak of war where his family had happened upon two men wearing Nazi armbands who were picketing a Jewish store and harassing anyone attempting to enter. His grandfather had defied the bullies, and one of them had grabbed him and shoved him aside, an act he would live to regret. Kurt's father had entered the altercation and dealt the Nazi a blow to the midsection that dispatched him to his knees. The other had had a notion to intervene, but one look at Kurt's father's sturdy physique was enough to repress his wavering courage. Kurt's mother had prompted them to flee for fear of reprisals from the detested Nazis. The incident had been imprinted indelibly in the young man's memory: the two men whom he held in highest regard had stood up to agents of the most pernicious regime ever released upon mankind.

Elena's appreciation for her new family deepened as she considered the strong character it had taken to stand up to the evil Nazi regime. She had learned that people had been sent off to concentration camps for less, never to be heard from again.

With the war over, Kurt's fascination with the Holocaust led him to read all he could on the subject. He learned that the mind-boggling mistreatment of the Jews had gotten worse with time. Truckloads had been rounded up and relocated to reservations in Poland, where the German people had been led to believe that Jews were treated favorably. Skilled laborers had been spared to be slowly worked to death while millions more waited their turn for the congested gas chambers and crematoriums.

Death's head contingents of the unprincipled SS had operated the rat-infested concentration camps with unmatched brutality. Under SS supervision, Jews and other undesirables had been methodically starved, battered, shot, or gassed. Hans Frank, the man overseeing the burgeoning Jewish problem in the Polish camps, had declared that, "The Jews must disappear," and disappear they did. Two million at Auschwitz, six million in total perished at the one hundred plus assembly line extermination sites throughout Europe. The fate of most Russian Jews at the hands of the genocidal SS squads had been simply to be marched into a field, stripped, shot in the head, and buried in a mass grave. Others had been herded onto cattle liners and sent by rail under the most barbaric conditions to their deaths in the Polish camps. There, as in various parts of Europe, modest numbers of Jews had led revolts and formed partisan bands to beleaguer the Nazis.

The slaughter of these innocents had gone entirely undisclosed to the German public to prevent precious morale from suffering at the ghastly reality that millions of human beings were being massacred in the name of racial purity.

As for the war's enduring effects, Kurt found in Elena a comforting soul mate who was able to ease his deepest afflictions of heart and mind and to see him through to a productive postwar experience. His family's love led to a rebirth mentally, spiritually, and psychologically, granting him a renewed passion for life.

Kurt called on Arie's mother in southern Bavaria, who welcomed him with open arms. She acknowledged having received his letter from Spain relating her son's loss, along with the letter Arie had given Kurt that last day in the trenches together, should one outlast the other. He sensed the understandable deep-seated anguish of her life's accumulated misfortune—trials far too weighty for most—as they spoke of Arie's unquestioned gallantry and thoughtfulness. She asked if he was doing all he could to bring Rykert to justice, and Kurt replied that he had been in contact with Allied authorities in hopes of tracking him down, if in fact he was still alive.

CHAPTER NINETEEN

May 1950. Five years since the merciful end to the worst debacle the human race had ever known; six years since that fateful summer day when Kurt and Elena escaped hell's fury and the devil's advocate and stole away into the safety of the Black Sea.

Kurt and Elena became the proud parents of three children. Albert had a little brother, Arie, and a baby sister, Katrina. Another child was well on its way. Kurt had entered into partnership with his father, farming the three hundred acres that had served their forefathers. They were poor—dirt poor—and hoping for a bountiful fall yield to offset their debts.

Seeing Elena running toward him, Kurt brought the tractor to a sudden stop. Panic was written in her eyes. His face mirrored the image as he leapt from the cab.

"Kurt, he has Albert! He has our son!"

"Who has Albert?" he asked.

"Rykert!"

Kurt gripped her shoulders. "Elena, control yourself! How do you know Rykert has our son?"

Stopping to catch her breath, she said, "The school headmaster just called. He said Albert was seen talking to a man with a scar on his cheek and then getting into his car. I've told them to alert the police."

Elena need say no more. Blood vessels hammering at his brain with the force of a thirty-pound sledgehammer and a wintry chill gripping his heart, Kurt bounded to the yard, rushed into the house to fetch his hunting rifle and revolver, and then vaulted into the truck to head off in blind pursuit of his adored son and his despicable birth-father.

"What are you doing?" Kurt demanded as Elena thrust open the passenger door.

Resembling a mama bear protecting her cub, she said, "I called over to your parents' to come look after the children. I'm going with you."

Kurt had no time to argue. He engaged the clutch and spun the tires to inaugurate their near-hopeless hunt. They had little to go on outside of their instincts, but he pressed the accelerator fully to the floor. Jumbled thoughts ricocheted haphazardly off the walls of his brain as they blew past a horse-drawn cart.

Tears welled in Elena's eyes as she sat deeply absorbed in her adopted son's welfare.

Driving flat-out with little concern for their own safety, Kurt said, "We'll never be free of this tyrant until I've seen him in his grave. And I vow to do just that."

"Where are we going?" she asked.

"To an airport. It's the only sensible alternative for Rykert. He'd dare not risk transporting Albert undercover by vehicle or public transport. He must have a private jet waiting at one of the local airports."

"Bremen?"

"No, too obvious. And in any case, I'm sure the police will alert every major carrier to that possibility. It's a stab in the dark, but I'm guessing an outlying airfield, some out-of-the-way two-bit runway—like the one on the road to Oldenburg. Are you with me?"

"Yes, go," she responded, throwing her head into her hands to beseech the Almighty for Albert's safekeeping.

They passed an oncoming police car with its lights flashing and siren screeching—undoubtedly in response to their son's abduction—giving them hope for their desperate situation.

How did the venomous wretch find out where they lived? They'd done all they could to keep their names out of registers, newspapers, and phonebooks, purposely remaining anonymous to all but those closest to them.

Kurt turned on a gravel road leading to the private airport and beheld a chilling sight: Albert being jostled aboard a twin-engine jet idling on the runway. Pressing the pedal to the floorboard, Kurt raced to intercept the plane as it taxied for takeoff.

Rykert realized at once who it was racing toward them and spurred the pilot on to what amounted to a deadly game of chicken, with neither willing to give ground.

Kurt sucked in a deep breath. One or the other must brake or veer to one side. He and Elena exchanged anguished glances, realizing that a head-on collision might kill them both, not to mention little Albert.

Finally, with not thirty meters separating them, the pilot lost his nerve and applied the brakes, swerving left of the runway. Kurt, too, slowed to avert a collision and instinctively reached for the rifle resting between them.

Suddenly, the side door swung open and Kurt beheld Rykert and another man discharging handguns at them, shattering glass and blowing their right rear tire.

Shouting at Elena to take cover, Kurt slammed the brakes and leapt from the truck to embrace his bolt-action rifle and repay deadly fire, mindful of Albert being aboard the plane. Advancing like a British dragoon, he scorned personal safety to see to his son's safe return.

Rykert's companion clutched his belly and tumbled from the craft, which had regained its forward motion.

With the clip spent, Kurt's hopes suffered setback. Reaching for his handgun, he was almost knocked from his feet by a blow to his lower right side; blood from a bullet wound stained his shirt. Regaining his balance, he ineffectually emptied his pistol at the wheels of the fleeing plane, wishing he'd been blessed with his old buddy Arie's unfailing accuracy.

As the plane gathered speed, Kurt and Elena looked on in horror as little Albert leapt out the open door, meeting up with the ground at better than sixty kilometers per hour. Sheer terror pervaded Kurt's senses as he sprinted to Albert's side, soon joined by a thoroughly distraught Elena.

The jet came to a full stop one hundred meters up the runway, and Kurt was conscious of Rykert running their way, pistol in hand. Survival instincts shouted at them to flee the scene, but their love for Albert propelled them on to inevitable death at the blackguard's hand.

They arrived to behold Albert's inanimate body crumpled on the runway, blood flowing from his nose and the bone of his lower right leg protruding through the skin. Elena propped his battered little head in her lap.

So in grief were they that they were largely indifferent to the mortal danger implicit in Rykert's presence. In a moment, he stood before them, pistol pointed squarely at Kurt's head. "How is he, Muller? Is he alive?"

Kneeling beside his adopted son, Kurt responded in a frosty voice, "He's still breathing, no thanks to you. You must have a medical kit in that plane, if you have any feelings for him."

Rykert hesitated a moment, deciding his course of action before turning back to the plane to carry out Kurt's request.

The distraught parents extended what comfort they could and were pleased to hear the sirens of police and ambulance crews, who must have been alerted by the airport staff.

Rykert reluctantly jumped into the aircraft, shut the door behind him, and bade his pilot flee the scene.

Kurt and Elena were not concerned about Rykert's capture; Albert had their undivided attention. It was when Elena directed his attention to the blood soaking up his shirt and pants about his right side that Kurt realized he had an urgent problem of his own. It was a glancing wound, but it had to be tended to prevent substantial blood loss.

The ambulance attendants saw to the wounded, while the police were left to bear the burden of Rykert's apprehension.

Albert remained in a coma for nearly a full day, during which time his badly broken body was restored to a measure of well-being.

Kurt recalled the first day he'd set eyes on the little guy in southern Ukraine, his tear-drenched eyes exposing the incalculable woe of his pitiable two-year existence. Scarcely six years later he was in a battle for his life, brought on by the very author of his birth. Kurt joyfully reflected on their delightful days together, fishing, hiking, playing soccer, or just relaxing before the grand, glowing fireplace while Kurt read him one of his favorite storybooks. They were thoroughly heartbroken and frequently in prayer over his delicate condition; still, they were invariably optimistic for a full recovery.

Kurt was resting in a chair with Elena half-asleep at the foot of Albert's bed when he came to. They rushed to embrace him as he took his swollen head in his hands and muttered incoherent sounds that to them were a splendid, full-symphony orchestra.

Within a few hours he was fully conscious, in much pain, and agonizing over the ordeal that had left him hopelessly disoriented. His family showered him with affection, but it was obvious his full recuperation was far off.

Kurt wondered what thoughts filled his tender little mind, hoping he had been blessed by God with amnesia over the barbarous incident. Such was not the case.

"Daddy," Albert said one day, when they were finally alone for a few precious moments in the hospital room. "That awful man who stole me away told me on the way to the airport that he's my real father…that he had to leave me for a time, but that he was now taking me away to live with him in South America. I know I was adopted by you and Mommy in Russia, but is that man my birth father?"

Kurt searched for an answer. He and Elena knew that Albert was just too young to deal with the truth of his parentage. "No, son. I fought against this man in the war, and he's only trying to get back at me by stealing you away. He'd say anything to hurt me, Albert. But we're going to catch him, and you'll never again have to worry about him snatching you away."

"Thank you, Daddy," he answered, cracking a wide smile for the first time in days, with visible relief upon his features after having bought Kurt's lie—at least for the time being.

CHAPTER TWENTY

Over a week passed, and Kurt gave up hope for Rykert's capture. Then one morning, as he sat sipping savory black coffee in Albert's room, a police officer burst in.

"We've found him, Muller," he said, "the man who tried to make off with your son. Airport officials in the Swiss ski village of Andermatt have made a positive identification of Rykert's plane. They've arrested his pilot and impounded the plane, and they are going through that town with a fine-tooth comb to find Rykert himself. If the pilot knows Rykert's whereabouts, he's not saying anything. But they should soon have Rykert in custody."

"Thank you, my friend, thank you very much," Kurt replied, setting his coffee down and rising to shake the officer's hand. "Andermatt, Switzerland?"

"That's the place."

"You've been most kind, and very helpful. Thank you again."

As the policeman departed, Kurt glanced at Elena and then at little Albert, who was heavily drugged and fast asleep.

Lying next to Albert, Elena propped herself up on an elbow and looked over at Kurt with those gorgeous brown eyes. "You're going after him, aren't you?"

Recognizing the anxiety in her face, Kurt ambled over to sit next to her on the bed, delicately kissing her forehead and taking her hands in his. "He got to us once, and he can get to us again. You must recognize the danger we're in here."

"Kurt, you heard what the doctor said. You came close to death only ten days ago. You're in no shape to go down there—and in any case, you're not needed. They've got him—you heard the man!"

"Elena, I've been given a clean bill of health, and I have no intentions of doing anything foolish. But I simply must be there to see this unconscionable maggot brought to justice. Now please trust me. Everything will be fine."

Following a brief moment of deliberation, she sat fully up in bed, drew a deep breath as if intending to carry on the debate, and then lowered her gaze and fell silent. She knew her husband's stubborn mind was made up.

Kurt drew her close for a tender farewell. As she bowed her head to shed her tears, he sensed that she understood his wanting to be a part of Rykert's capture. He must be there, bandaged or not, to see him put away once and for all. Surely Arie could not rest peacefully in his grave, and surely Albert would never be safe, so long as this monster remained at large. Rykert was a criminal, a fugitive from justice who deserved capture and execution. Furthermore, he posed a very real threat to Kurt's young family.

Kurt caught a late evening flight to Geneva, followed by a red-eye to Zurich. From there he rented a car to Andermatt.

It was mid-morning when he pulled into the picturesque little town. A brisk north wind united with a steady drizzle to chill the crisp mountain air. He asked directions to the police station and made his way there.

If Kurt's thoughts could kill, Rykert would've been dead a thousand times over, but it now seemed only a matter of time before justice was served. He realized that the emotion had gone out of the conflict. He felt strangely devoid of any hate or revenge. Seeing to the end of Captain Gerd Rykert had become a plain and simple matter of doing what was right, no different from the dispassionate putting down of a dangerous animal for the common good.

The officer at the station's front desk had little to offer Kurt. "Yes, less than an hour ago we made an attempt to apprehend this Rykert fellow at the Eagle's Nest Villas," the man said, "but he appeared to have been tipped off to our coming. He wounded one of our men with his pistol and left the other unconscious at the villas. We know nothing more than that at this time, but I assure you we have every available man on the case."

"The Eagle's Nest Villas?" Kurt asked. "How can I get there from here?"

Pointing out the window, he replied, "You'd follow this road straight north, about a kilometer. And may I ask what business this is of yours, sir?"

Kurt ignored the question, bounding out the door en route to the villas. Stopping with a screech of the tires, Kurt took the pistol from his overnight bag, concealed it beneath his jacket, and raced into the villas. A gaunt and spindly man greeted him at the front desk. "Yes, sir. How may I be of service?"

"I need some information on one of your guests, the one who shot the policeman and ran off."

The man asked, "Are you with the police, sir? If so, I must see some identification."

"No...no, I'm not with the police, but I am involved in the hunt for the man who shot the officer. I desperately need your help. Please."

An older, creamy-complexioned gentleman with a round fleshy face and beer-keg body wrapped in a tailored suit emerged from a fancy office. "I'll take it from here, Henri," he stated, leading Kurt into his office.

Kurt cordially extended his hand. "Muller, Kurt Muller, sir."

"Hermann Franck. By your dialect, I take it you're not from these parts," he commented, shaking hands before closing the door behind them.

"Oh, no sir. I'm from northern Germany, and I have a very great interest in helping see to the capture of the man who shot the policeman. Have you any idea where he has gone? I understand they've impounded his plane, so he'll be driving or on foot."

Franck turned to pour brandy into a pair of shot glasses and then handed one to Kurt, his free hand fingering the desktop. He lifted his glass and threw back his head, flinching just a bit upon impact. "Well, it seems that this Rykert, or Buhler as he went by in this establishment, was tipped off about the police and stole off a bit ahead of schedule."

Kurt's eyes thinned out. "Have you any idea where he might be headed?"

Franck waddled to a sizable aquarium teeming with brightly colored fish and asked rather indifferently, "Are you fond of these little creatures, Mr. Muller?"

"Well...uh, no sir. I...I can't say I have any particular feeling for them."

Faintly rocking on his feet, Franck said, "I'm quite fascinated with them myself. In fact, I must confess to having quite an obsession. But you know, they can at times be a very great bore, slowly swimming about, putting me half to sleep—until I feed them, that is." Franck shook a bit of fish food into the murky water and looked on in amusement at the ensuing frenzy. "You know, we humans can be a bit like that ourselves: totally inactive until we are adequately stimulated. And then it's really quite remarkable just how cooperative we can be. I'm sure you understand what I am getting at, Mr. Muller. I do indeed have information on your man and would be quite happy to share it with you, if you choose to cooperate."

Kurt's countenance dropped as he became wise to this avaricious little slime. "I understand," he remarked, reaching for a handful of Swiss currency in his pocket.

As Kurt offered the money, Franck waved him off with a sneer, his gelatinous, fat face jiggling with the exuberant shake of his head. "No, my friend, I don't think you understand at all. I said adequately stimulated, not made a fool of."

Resisting a strong craving to reach out and beat the scum-sucking degenerate half to death, Kurt flashed a furrowed brow. "Mr. Franck, I assure you I am not a bounty hunter being paid an outlandish fee to apprehend this man. I fought with the German army during the last war and saw him commit heinous crimes against the Jewish people. Just last week, he seriously injured my son in an attempt to abduct him. I'm not a rich man—far from it. I know I could never meet your price. I ask you, sir, as a gentleman, to give me the information so that I may help the police apprehend this madman."

His eyes those of a viper, Franck shrugged. "Tsk, tsk. Very touching. Very touching indeed, soldier. But you see, as an unabashed supporter of your country's just cause in the last war, I am none too disposed to offer gratuitous favors to Jew lovers. Truth be told, I find Mr. Rykert's so-called heinous crimes quite palatable. Furthermore, I couldn't give the smallest crap for that son of yours." He turned to feed his fish. "Money talks, Mr. Muller. When you have raised sufficient capital to cause me to turn on this Nazi, do come back and see me, won't you?"

With an expression more like that of his old buddy Arie, Kurt slapped his untouched brandy on the desk and lunged with uncharacteristic fury, inflicting a blow to Franck's lower back, then grabbed his arm and thrust it up behind him. Clutching the thinning hair on the back of his head with his right hand, Kurt plunged him face-first into the fish tank, bringing him up seconds later. "Adequately stimulated yet?" he asked.

Uttering unbounded profanity and bleating like a stuck pig, with red-rimmed eyes about to pop out of his rage-reddened face, Franck gasped, "I'll have you arrested!"

Kurt forced him back under.

The second time up, Franck was not nearly so belligerent. He had, in fact, acquired a distinctly respectful tone. Gasping, he said, "All right…all right, I'll talk."

"And for your sake, it had better be the truth, or I'll be back for you."

Gasping in Kurt's firm grasp, Franck started up. "He offered to pay me…a sum of money…should I alert him to any…police activity…with regard to his capture. Sure enough, they came asking…about a man of his description whose plane they had seized. They had all roads blocked…in and out of town. When I informed him of this, he paid me…as promised. With the roads blocked, he knew it would be hopeless to try to escape by car...so he planned to hike off through the mountain pass...directly to the north."

"And then what?"

"That's it. What more do you want?"

Kurt drove Franck's fat head under once again, bringing him up seconds later.

His face cadaverous, coughing and gasping for air, he indeed had something to share. "All right...enough already! I'll...I'll tell you what you want...Just let me...catch my breath."

"Go on."

"He gave me another check to drive my car...my Volkswagen van...to a place on the far side of the mountain, away from the roadblocks...to leave it parked with the keys under the seat...so that he could make good his escape from there. I was about to leave when you arrived."

"Where exactly on the far side of the mountain were you to leave this vehicle?" Kurt demanded, wrenching his arm a little farther up his back.

"There's a campground...not ten minutes' drive up the highway...straight north from here...you can't miss it...I'm to have the van parked there within the hour."

Releasing his grip, Kurt asked for the keys to the van, which Franck grudgingly handed over while restoring himself to some semblance of order.

His voice lacking the earlier bravado, he asked, "Do you really think you can get away with manhandling me like this, and then stealing my vehicle on top of it?"

Kurt reached for the check on Franck's desk and replied, "Oh yes, Mr. Franck, I do. I'll keep Rykert's check as insurance against your running off to the police to tell them stories that may land me in any difficulty. I'd imagine they would not be too pleased to learn that a member of their own was seriously wounded as the result of your having alerted Rykert to their plans to apprehend him. You'll find the check back here inside the van when my work is done. Understood?"

Franck nodded his sopping head.

Kurt turned to exit the room, check and keys in hand, hoping once and for all to end his pitiful life-and-death struggle with Rykert. He rushed to the van, noting that his scuffle with Franck had reopened his side wound. Engaging the key and turning over the engine, he glanced up at the mountain pass, which Rykert must have been nearly half-through.

CHAPTER TWENTY-ONE

Kurt's heart raced as he wound his way to the back side of the mountain. He soon came upon the campsite, largely abandoned due to the inclement weather. The day was beastly gray, utterly sunless front to back with dark cloud bands threatening a downpour.

He parked the van and left its front windows open in a secluded area. Then he fashioned a hideaway for himself a few steps into the brush. With great satisfaction, he awaited the climactic conclusion to his private war with SS Captain Gerd Rykert. His mind was subjected to an anxiety reminiscent of his heady days on the Eastern Front, particularly the painful memories of his fright-filled flight from the insidious SS.

A crow momentarily perched on a limb nearby caught sight of Kurt before flittering off with a high-pitched squawk. Soon after, a pair of chattering red squirrels dashed past, pausing for an instant to consider the trespasser before they vaulted to the asylum of a towering pine. Otherwise, Kurt was alone with his thoughts.

About half an hour later, Kurt heard the snapping of branches and the labored lumbering of heavy feet. All was unfolding according to plan. He watched his great antagonist approach the van at a gallop, panting and horribly strained, his chest heaving.

His face flushed and his hair tousled by the brisk wind, Rykert drew a deep breath and opened the door to begin his fruitless search for the ignition key. At first carefully, but then madly, he looked everywhere—under the seat, in the glove compartment, in the back—cursing like a sailor. Little did he realize the key was the least of his worries. His day of reckoning had arrived.

Kurt drew his revolver and approached the van, jingling the keys. "Would you be looking for these, Captain Rykert? Mr. Franck regrets that he cannot be here personally. Something about having to rush into town to cash a large foreign check. Now, if you'll be so good as to step out of the vehicle, unbuckle your holster, and raise your hands, I just may not be forced to blow your scurvy head clean off your shoulders."

Startled, his face turned cold. With much of the haughtiness gone from his voice, Rykert replied, "You had your chance to shoot me dead on the Russian seacoast, and you couldn't do it then, Muller. Why should I believe you now?"

Kurt gave him a hard look, his face flushing with indignation. "Motivation. I lacked suitable motivation. But with your attack on my family last week, I assure you that has all changed now. You'd do well to play along."

"My son, Muller. How is he?" he asked as he stepped from the van and dropped his holster.

"You have no son, Rykert. And now that you bring it up, I seriously doubt you ever had much of a father."

"All right then, *your* son. Is he alive?"

Kurt replied with a scalding glare, "He's alive, but badly hurt. And he's seen the last of you. You can bet your life on that."

"Yes, I should imagine. Now listen to me, Muller. I'll tell you just what I'm going to do. I'm going to walk straight off into those trees. Shoot me in the back if you are able, but I'm betting you're still too much the honorable gentleman for that. If you think I'm going to accompany you to some Swiss jail to be extradited for an unjust hanging, then you've got another thought coming, my friend."

Kurt directed a warning shot one pace ahead of Rykert, prompting the fugitive's final appeal, his expression and voice revealing his growing insecurity.

"Muller, I have untold wealth in Paraguay. You can have it—all of it—along with my word I'll never again disturb you or your loved ones, if you'll just let me drive out of here today. Just think about your family living in such wretched poverty on that miserable little farm of yours."

"You really are pathetic, Rykert. You know that, don't you? To how many of your wartime victims did you extend such mercy?"

Rykert raised his hands and stepped toward the trees, blurting, "You have no authority to use that weapon in this country, Muller. Go ahead and shoot. They'll hang you for murder."

"The way I look at it, with you dead and gone, there'll be one less wart on the ass of society, which may just justify my own demise. Now stop, I warn you!" Kurt shouted, discharging a bullet into the ground at Rykert's feet before tossing aside the pistol and lunging after him.

Rykert turned just as Kurt leapt to bring him down, the two crashing heavily like toppled trees. Kurt felt a terrible pain from the wound in his right side and was jolted by a forearm smash which sent him sprawling. Rykert pounced like a cat, but Kurt pushed him away with bent knees. Up on their feet, Kurt landed a pair of punches, but a vicious left hook to the chin sent him reeling. Blood took to the air as they exchanged several staggering shots—a knock-down, drag-'em-out, life-and-death slugfest.

Noticing Kurt's bloodied side, Rykert delivered the bout's most telling blow.

Kurt fell back, and blood flowed from the wound. As Rykert sprang to build on his advantage, Kurt summoned all his energy to kick at his adversary's left leg, dislocating the kneecap and sending him sprawling in agony. Kurt brought down his left fist to open a sizable cut, propelling his opponent face-first to the ground.

Beaten and bloodied, his left cheek gashed and spewing blood, the punch-drunk Rykert looked up at Kurt as one having been deeply wronged, the quintessence of wide-eyed innocence.

Kurt dragged his pain-drenched adversary to the van and tied him to the bench seat in back with a length of tow rope for the trip to the Andermatt police station. He considered that this pitiful soul was assuredly possessed of the diabolic demons of which his grandfather had spoken from the pulpit. He had, of his own free will, bid them come govern his heart, and they had eagerly obliged, unbinding a ghastly iniquity.

Back at the villas, Kurt parked as per his agreement with Franck. He tore the check to shreds before leaving it, as promised, safe within the van. He had the desk clerk call for the police, who presently relieved Kurt of his prisoner.

Kurt drove to the airport at peace with his world, knowing his family members were finally free from the fear of this awful man ever coming back into their lives.

EPILOGUE

▼

Upon extradition to the state of Israel to stand trial for his abominable crimes, SS Colonel Gerd Rykert—he'd been twice promoted in the last months of the war—was hanged on a cold, clear December afternoon. That same day, Kurt took his adopted son, Albert, on a special trip for one of the most important talks of the boy's life. To much of the outside world, the announcement of Rykert's execution was barely newsworthy, but to Kurt and his family, it was a red-letter day.

Kurt and Albert still needed some time together to discuss the youngster's true heritage. Kurt knew he could no longer keep from him the dark secret. Albert would soon escape the gullible innocence of youth. Better to come out with it now and be done with it. Though the legitimate progeny of a shockingly malicious and remorseless criminal, he was their son in every sense of the word, as much a part of them as their birth-children. It was up to Kurt to communicate that to him this day, if indeed it needed saying.

But how to tell him? Once again, the words of Ecclesiastes came to Kurt's mind. "There is a time for everything: a time to be born and a time to die; a time to plant and a time to harvest; a time to kill and a time to heal; a time to grieve and a time to dance; a time for scattering stones and a time for gathering stones; a time to embrace and a time not to embrace; a time to find and a time to lose; a time for keeping and a time for throwing away; a time to tear and a time to repair; a time to be quiet and a time to speak up; a time for loving and a time for hating; a time for war and a time for peace."

And, as the result of his exacting experience with Rykert, Kurt came to realize one more truth: there is a time for duty and a time for honor.

The End

978-0-595-39683-2
0-595-39683-6

Printed in the United States
64752LVS00004B/253-258